SUSHAM BEDI was born i
studied at Delhi University a
As a teenager she became a l
All India Radio and later on
school and won many award:
undergraduate but her writin
when her first story was published in the literary magazine
Kahani. Susham Bedi's first novel, *Havan* (*The Fire Sacrifice*), was
serialised in the magazine *Ganga* and published as a novel in
1989. It was published in Urdu in 1992. Since then she has
published two more novels, *Lautna* or *The Returning* (1992) and
Itar or *The Other* (1992). All three deal with the problems and
cultural dilemmas of Indians living in the West. Susham Bedi
taught in Delhi and Punjab Universities until 1975 when she
followed her husband to Brussels where she became a
correspondent for the Times of India. She has lived in the
United States since 1979 and has been teaching in Hindi
Language and Literature at Columbia University in New York
since 1985.

DAVID RUBIN has a Ph.D. in comparative literature from
Columbia University, where he has taught Indian literature and
Hindi. He has translated several volumes of Hindi and Nepali
fiction and poetry. Among his other publications are novels,
short stories, and *After The Raj*, a critical study of British fiction
about the sub-continent in the years following Indian
independence.

SUSHAM BEDI

THE FIRE SACRIFICE

(HAVAN)

Translated from the Hindi by
David Rubin

HEINEMANN

Heinemann Educational
A Division of Heinemann Publishers (Oxford) Ltd
Halley Court, Jordan Hill, Oxford OX2 8EJ

Heinemann: A Division of Reed Publishing (USA) Inc.
361 Hanover Street, Portsmouth, NH 03801–3912, USA

Heinemann Educational Books (Nigeria) Ltd
PMB 5205, Ibadan
Heinemann Educational Boleswa
PO Box 10103, Village Post Office, Gaborone, Botswana

FLORENCE   PRAGUE   PARIS   MADRID
ATHENS   MELBOURNE   JOHANNESBURG
AUCKLAND   SINGAPORE   TOKYO
CHICAGO   SAO PAULO

First published in India under the title
Havan by Parag Praleashan in 1989

© Susham Bedi 1989
This translation © David Rubin 1993
First published by Heinemann Educational in 1993

Series Editor: Ranjana Sidhanta Ash

British Library Cataloguing in Publication Data
A catalogue record for this book is available from the British Library.

Cover design by Touchpaper
Cover illustration by Mike Bennion

ISBN 0435 95087 8

Phototypeset by Cambridge Composing (UK) Ltd, Cambridge
Printed and bound in Great Britain
by Cox & Wyman Ltd, Reading, Berkshire

93 94   10 9 8 7 6 5 4 3 2 1

Introduction to the Asian Writers Series

Heinemann's new Asian Writers Series, aided by the Arts Council of Great Britain, intends to introduce English language readers to some of the interesting fiction written in languages that most will neither know nor study.

For too long popular acclaim for Asian writing in the West has been confined to the handful of authors who choose to write in English rather than in the language of their own cultures. Heinemann's entry into the field should dispel this narrow perspective and place modern Asian writing within the broad spectrum of contemporary world literature.

The first six works selected for the series are translations of novels from five languages: Bengali, Hindi, Malayalam, Tamil and Urdu. The six novels span seventy-five years of change in the subcontinent. *Quartet*, one of Rabindranath Tagore's most skilfully constructed and lively classics, was first published in 1916, whereas the most recent work chosen, *The Fire Sacrifice*, was written by the up-and-coming Hindi novelist Susham Bedi and first published in 1989.

These first six titles face the normal problems affecting literature in translation, not least the difficulty of establishing an exact parallel of the thought or verbal utterance of the original in the target language. When the source text is in a non-European language and embodies a culture and literary style quite alien to English language readers, the translator's task is made even more difficult.

Susan Bassnett in her invaluable work on translation studies describes the typical colonial attitude to the literature of the colonised as a 'master and servant' relationship, with the European translator attempting to 'improve' and 'civilise' the source text. At the other end of the scale she describes a kind of 'cannibalism' in which the translator almost 'devours' the text to disgorge a totally new product. Fortunately, the translators of this series fall into neither category but manage to retain a balanced view of their craft.

While it is very important to produce a translation that uses a style both readable and engaging to an English language readership, it must not obscure the particularities of literary devices, figures of speech, and aesthetic detail that the author uses to convey his or her sensibility, imagination and verbal artistry. Should such faithfulness to the original produce in the English version a greater degree of sentiment or charged imagery than the reader might expect, one hopes that he or she will be ready to accept the novelty of writing from an unfamiliar source.

In publishing the Asian Writers Series, Heinemann is taking a bold step into an area which has been neglected for too long. It is our hope that readers will respond with interest and enthusiasm as they discover the outstanding quality of these novels.

RANJANA SIDHANTA ASH, SERIES EDITOR, 1993

Introduction to *The Fire Sacrifice*

Susham Bedi's first novel, *The Fire Sacrifice*, is in the tradition of social realism in Hindi fiction that began with Premchand about the time of the First World War. Premchand and his contemporaries in other regional languages devoted most of their attention to the problems of the underprivileged, but in the period following Indian Independence in 1947 novelists have been more preoccupied with the middle classes, their alienation, and the tension between modernisation and conservative religious values. Susham Bedi brings her own originality to bear on the tradition, both by treating the particular problems and cultural conflicts of Indians who have migrated to the West and by developing a technique in which realistic observation is tempered by psychological subtlety.

The Fire Sacrifice was published in 1989 both in book form and in a serialised magazine version. *Havan*, the Hindi title of the novel, is the name of an ancient sacrificial ritual performed on auspicious occasions and for purification. It acquired great importance from the Arya Samaj movement founded by Swami Dayananda Sarasvati in 1875. The Arya Samaj, to which Mrs Bedi's family belongs, advocated a reformed Hinduism based on its Vedic origins, and emphasised ethical principles, the equality of women, and the rejection of untouchability and child marriage.

Guddo, the heroine of *The Fire Sacrifice*, is profoundly influenced by Dayananda's teachings but is nevertheless both a sensual and an ambitious woman. As an attractive widow she is extremely vulnerable, especially in the emigré Indian community of Westernised doctors and other professionals in New York, where

vii

Indian conventions may be more easily ignored than in India. In her struggle to provide education and opportunities for her son and two daughters, Guddo makes many sacrifices, working in menial positions and living in a sordid flat to economise; but, as she comes to realise, she also sacrifices her principles, using her affair with an Indian doctor not only for his help in finding positions for her children but also, though she is loath to admit it, for her own gratification.

There is a satirical undercurrent in the depiction of the affluent New York Indian community, with their lip-service to Hindu ideals and their tax-deductible contributions for the construction of more and more new temples. Guddo's two sons-in-law, both doctors, are conceited and materialistic; in their public lives they appear thoroughly Americanised but at home they expect their wives, who have their own professional careers, to remain completely subservient.

Ultimately the implicit question remains unanswered: is it possible to remain genuinely Indian and survive in the West? Testing the problem, *The Fire Sacrifice* presents a wide range of Indian personalities, Hindu and Muslim, doctors, lawyers and taxi-drivers, coping with discrimination, home-sickness and bewilderment. Guddo, with a master's degree and a teaching certificate, must work in a newspaper stall and later as a salesgirl; one of her brothers-in-law, formerly a well-to-do mine manager, becomes a doorman. Indians marry Americans, and both Indians and Americans become victims of the other. Guddo succeeds in her driving ambition to bring prosperity to her children but at the novel's end happiness still eludes her.

Beyond giving us a dramatic and compassionate account of the problems of Indians trying to make a new life abroad, *The Fire Sacrifice*, like all good fiction, reminds us of the universality of human nature and the common experience of people no matter how divergent their origins and cultures.

DAVID RUBIN, 1993

A Note on the Translation

Readers who compare the English translation with the original Hindi will find that the two do not in all instances accord exactly; this is because Susham Bedi made a few revisions and abridgements in her text while preparing it for translation. The translator is grateful to her and to Professor Frances Pritchett of Columbia University for many helpful suggestions in the course of this undertaking. A Glossary may be found on page 181.

*To my mother Shrimati Shantidevi Dhamija
and
my father Ishvardas Dhamija*

One

'*Prajapate na tvadetanyanyo vishva jatani pari ta babhuva yatkamaste juhumastanno astu vayam syama patayo rayinam . . .*' While she chants the *mantra* Guddo keeps pondering its meaning: 'All-pervading Lord of the universe! Whatever the objects or goals we pray for, taking refuge in you, let our desires be fulfilled . . .' Remembering what she had prayed for, what she had desired, Guddo glances around at the members of her family gathered in the room.

Today, the first day of the new year, is full of joy for Guddo. She was brought up to believe that if the first day should be a happy one the rest of the year would pass without troubles. And so she has planned the fire sacrifice in her apartment today.

Her sister Gita said, 'How can you perform a fire sacrifice in an apartment? The whole place will fill up with smoke, then the fire alarm will go off, and don't forget the wall-to-wall carpeting.'

But Guddo answered, 'I've seen a fire sacrifice done in Juneja's mother's place. There wasn't any problem. All you have to do is spread aluminium foil on the rug and put a big cast iron pan on it for the fire-pit. You can get the kindling and all the other things you need from the Gujarati grocer. Anyway, I've already ordered a fire-pit from somebody at the New York Arya Samaj. It's expensive, of course – thirty dollars, he said. But the thing is, you can get everything right here in the city.'

Guddo has invited both her daughters, along with Anuj, her son-in-law, and her two sisters with their children and Satinder, her brother-in-law. She came to this city over ten years ago but today is the first time she's had a chance, to say nothing of the courage, to perform the sacrifice. It seems to her that this is the

1

first moment she's had to sit and catch her breath since she came here.

*

In the beginning it was her younger sister, Pinki, who told her she ought to come to New York. Pinki emigrated about seventeen years ago; Satinder, her husband, came first, right after their engagement, and was able to send for her three years later. While he went on studying he eventually found a job for himself. In those days it was still fairly easy to get work, but Jijaji, Gita's husband, used to carp at him. 'What's the point of all that studying?' he would say. 'With two MAs and a PhD he can only teach people whose second language is English. And he doesn't earn very much, either. If only he'd become a doctor or an engineer, well . . .'

But Pinki's letters were so full of enthusiasm, brimming over with praise for the wonders of America, that anybody who read them would long to catch a plane and fly over on the spot. 'Guddo, sister, you wouldn't believe the wealth and luxury here! When they say the rivers are flowing with milk, well, it's really true. Everything's so cheap you don't have to worry about the price. In India it's a big decision whether to put butter on the toast or not, but here *everything* is cooked in butter. And the orange and apple juice, you can drink it to your heart's content. There's no shortage of *anything*!'

When Pinki left India she'd been as skinny as a broomstraw. But when after three years in America, she came back on holiday for the first time, how fair her skin had become! Her cheeks were pink as roses, her figure had filled out beautifully, she radiated health and well-being. And of course everybody in the family was buzzing about her, she was invited and welcomed every-where. And she'd brought a vast amount of baggage stuffed with gifts – bright flower-print parasols, American pastel georgette and chiffon saris, transistors and hair-dryers, lipstick and nail-polish, lotions and wrinkle-removing creams, after-shaves, colognes – something, in short, for everybody in the family. And as Guddo looked at Pinki's beautiful soft sweaters and listened to

2

the tales of that foreign paradise, how she had yearned to get all of it for herself! Then, unexpectedly, fate took an abrupt turn that made it seem impossible for her not to come to America: quite suddenly her husband fell ill and died. Guddo's life was turned upside down.

She had earned her BA degree but before completing her MA she was married to the boy her father had chosen for her, a well-settled young engineer. Now all of a sudden he was gone, and her father too was dead. With the help of her brothers and her husband's friends she somehow managed to go on to get her teaching certificate and find a job in a local school. Then, within two years of her husband's death, with money from the Provident Fund and loans, she started construction of a house built on land they'd bought during the early days of their marriage.

When the house was finished Guddo rented out the back part to augment her limited teacher's income and improve the quality of her life. She would have liked to send the three children to a convent school but could not afford the fees. So she enrolled only the little boy, while the girls entered a government school. They were both bright and able, and the younger was always the first in her class. As for Guddo herself, she began to study for a master's degree in English while she continued teaching.

Pinki kept on writing to her, telling her she simply had to come to America. There she would be able to earn many times the money and have the children study in really excellent schools; on the other hand, so long as she continued working as a teacher in India she'd always be hard up for money. At first Guddo was in a quandary about it. She wondered if there was any point in uprooting herself from her settled domestic life. Then too, she'd probably be a burden on Pinki in New York. Biji (as she called her mother) and her brothers advised her not to abandon her stable, comfortable existence, especially since they had all worked so hard to get her on her feet after the tragedy.

But her elder brother's wife had a different view. She said sarcastically, 'If you go to America at least you'll get rich – but if you don't, you'll always be pestering everybody else here for help. Don't forget, you've got two daughters to marry off.'

3

Guddo was hurt, of course, and realised how much her sister-in-law was fed up with doing things for her. If she went abroad at least her brother's family would be freed from their responsibility. After all, who wants to have to put up with a widowed sister-in-law?

But Biji disagreed. 'There's nothing for you in America,' she said. 'You'll only be a burden on your younger sister.'

Guddo knew perfectly well that Biji was just worried about the inconvenience to Pinki and the possibility that Guddo would take advantage of the good-hearted girl. She also knew that behind her back Biji was saying, 'Guddo's always been given the best of everything because she's the eldest and still she's got her hand out all the time. How much do we have to keep doing for her? Why doesn't she settle for what she already has? Why does she keep sponging on her brothers and sisters? There's no reason at all for her to go and move in with Pinki . . .'

But there was a special bond between Guddo and Pinki. As the oldest child in the family Guddo had practically brought up Pinki, the youngest, and when she was only ten she'd carry her around with her everywhere. Later she always took Pinki's side in the disputes with her sister and brothers. Always soft-spoken with Pinki, always affectionate, Guddo never beat her, unlike Gita, the middle sister, who would slap her over any trifle. Guddo recalled how once when Pinki, coming home from playing, had climbed with her dirty feet onto Gita's freshly made-up bed, Gita struck her all over her body. Pinki cried for hours. That night Guddo took her to sleep in her bed. After that, Pinki often came to sleep with her. At mealtimes, because she was the eldest, Guddo was the one who served the food for everyone; when they had the younger girl's favourite okra or mashed eggplant Pinki would set a stool next to Guddo and stare at the dish with longing eyes until Guddo, after serving her father and brothers, would give the biggest portion to Pinki. So it was no surprise that Pinki would always do whatever her sister asked. Now she had even sent Guddo the ticket for her and Raju, her son, to come to America.

Years before, after she married and went to her husband's

4

home, Guddo had again found herself the eldest of the daughters and daughters-in-law. This meant she was constantly burdened with the problems of her husband's five brothers and sisters. She quickly learned that she was expected to get them educated and married off and, in fact, devote her whole life to looking after them. And they didn't mind sponging off her, if she gave them the chance. Bubbu, the middle brother-in-law, wanted to come and study in the city where Guddo lived. Alarmed, she wrote back at once that he had no chance of being accepted at the city school. Fortunately, it turned out that he actually was refused admission, otherwise God knows how many years she would have had him on her hands. And then, think of all the money she'd had to send for her fault-finding sister-in-law's wedding! Even afterwards the girl still complained because Guddo and Premkumar, her husband, didn't come to the wedding – for they knew that if they did it would cost them even more. And there were still three more sisters-in-law to be married off. So, since she knew there would be no pleasing her in-laws no matter what she did, Guddo began to ignore them.

But she learned the cost of this strategy after her husband's death when the in-laws declared themselves quite unable to give her any financial help or even moral support. Furthermore, she had also made the mistake of letting Mantu, her own brother, stay with her a few months while he took a course – they would never forgive her for that.

Guddo was more and more alone. She no longer felt the same attachment to her brothers and sisters, and after Premkumar's death nothing in life really meant much to her any more except for her three children.

Then, four years later, she finally got the chance she'd been waiting for, to go to America. The red tape over green card and passport didn't bother her at all, but it broke her heart to leave her two daughters at their boarding schools to finish their studies – Anima, the elder, doing her BSc in chemistry, while Tanima went on in a pre-med programme. But there was no help for it.

Two

While she and Raju rode from John F Kennedy airport in a taxi with Pinki and Satinder, Guddo did not feel the kind of excitement, the indescribable joy, she had experienced so many times before in her imagination. On the contrary, when she saw the city's towering buildings of hard stone she was aware of a strange sadness, a feeling of suffocation. 'This part of town,' Pinki told her, 'is called Manhattan.'

Pinki's ground-floor one-bedroom apartment was in the very heart of Manhattan, right across the street from a fashion boutique and a bookstore. Until late at night the whole neighbourhood seemed to be holding a noisy carnival, so Pinki always kept the apartment windows shut tight, with thick curtains drawn. If you ever drew them back for even a second the eyes of nosy passers-by invaded the room. In the stuffy apartment the stale smell of Indian spices and fried food permeated everything – curtains, carpets, bedding, people. As that smell spread with the central heating Guddo, anxious and nauseated, felt that it would suffocate her. The only relief she found was from sticking her head out of the bathroom window, which opened on a closed court, and filling her lungs with fresh air.

Pinki took a couple of days off work to give Guddo a tour of the city: Statue of Liberty, Empire State Building, World Trade Center, United Nations . . . Pinki's apartment was on Twelfth Street, near New York University, in a part of town called Greenwich Village. Because so many artists lived there and because of the free ways of the university students, the area was considered very bohemian.

Pinki also introduced her to all sorts of popular American foods. Raju was in heaven enjoying pizza, hamburgers, hot dogs, and ice cream made in thirty different flavours.

Pinki's son, Arjun, resented not being included in these sightseeing expeditions because he was at school. Guddo soon found there were other problems. Satinder, Pinki's husband, who spent most of his free time doing research, was worried because he hadn't been offered a tenured post at the university where he taught, so he had the additional burden of having to look for a new teaching job. Pinki was afraid that if he didn't find it soon they wouldn't be able to get by on her salary alone.

One year before Guddo's arrival, Gita, the middle sister, had come to New York with her family. Conditions at home had become so hopeless that, following the example of other Indians with relatives in America, Gita decided that the only possible solution to her problems was to join Pinki. Jijaji, her husband, had been wiped out by the nationalisation of his coal mines. Though he tried his hand at various other jobs nothing worked out. Even the land he had bought earlier for farming, thought at the time to be a good investment, turned out to be a total loss when the government appropriated it for Sanjay Gandhi's small-car manufacturing project and paid much less than it was worth in compensation. With no other source of income available and the family savings used up for daily household expenses, Gita wrote to Pinki to see what she could suggest. Pinki had already applied for American citizenship and would soon be getting it. As soon as she learned of Gita's money troubles, she enthusiastically took on the responsibility of sponsoring her sister's family. In times like these that's what brothers and sisters are for, she thought. She promptly sent off the necessary papers, and within a year Gita, Jijaji, and their three children were living in Pinki's one-bedroom apartment.

For Jijaji it meant starting his life all over again. The coal mines were an inheritance and he had never had any training in business management. In those days it was considered more than enough if you studied through the Intermediate level. He had felt no need – or desire – for further education. But things were

7

different in America, where you couldn't just start a business from scratch, without the capital or, for that matter, the courage. Having failed so many times, by now he had lost all his self-confidence and for the first time he began to feel inferior because he wasn't an engineer or a doctor. Encouraged by Pinki and Satinder, he started selling Indian brass figures and ready-made clothes every Saturday and Sunday at a flea-market on a Greenwich Village sidewalk. Other Indians were already there peddling similar cheaply made objects. Samples of folk art from other third-world countries were also on sale nearby – wooden statues from Africa, jade and other semi-precious stones from Mexico, various kinds of jewelry, Uruguayan leather handbags. Gita and Jijaji would fill suitcases with out-of-date wares bought from Indian wholesalers and bring them to the market. Jijaji felt so ashamed of having to sell things on the sidewalk that tears actually came to his eyes; if any Indian walked by and saw him he would pray for the earth to open and swallow him. When she realised this, Gita told him, 'If it distresses you so much, why go on with it?' But of course, for the moment, there was nothing else.

Months went by. Pinki, who once had longed for her brothers and sisters, began to regret inviting Gita and her family. The children were constantly fighting. If anything was misplaced they would blame one another, and often they even quarrelled over their food. Gita's son Ashok complained that Pinki ordered things like Danish cheese from outside for Arjun because he'd been brought up 'to eat American', but *he* had to eat dal and vegetables. Gita tried not to make too much of such things but all the same everybody, shut up in the tiny apartment, was getting on one another's nerves. The former harmony of the household vanished and resentment steadily increased between the two families.

The two brothers-in-law were not getting along either. Jijaji wanted to talk about nothing but his schemes for making money, while Satinder had no taste for such small talk; he had his own circle of professors and scholars and spent most of his time away from the house with them – something else to make Pinki angry.

But for her part, working a full day in a library and commuting three hours a day, she had little leisure for worrying about such matters. Her ambition was to become the director of the library eventually and she gave everything to her job. When Arjun was only a year old she had enrolled in a master's programme in library science. Early every morning she would leave him at a child-care centre and then go on to work.

After many setbacks, Jijaji finally found a job as a doorman in a luxury apartment building. In the beginning he had considered such work beneath him but when nothing else worked out he felt that his job offered him his only chance at earning a salary. Gita too found a position as a temporary substitute in a child care centre. By then almost a year had gone by, and as soon as Gita was earning a salary, she and her family, exasperated by the constant bickering, found an apartment for themselves in an inexpensive area far from Manhattan. Worn out, Pinki did nothing to stop them from moving. By Indian standards, this was shockingly rude, but at this point Pinki no longer cared.

Nor did she feel much like having Guddo join her either so soon after Gita's family had left. But this was precisely the moment when Guddo, invited long before, was all set to come. So Pinki enjoyed only a brief rest from Gita and her family, with all their complaining and arguing. All the same, when Guddo finally arrived, Pinki's happiness knew no bounds.

Three

Guddo had brought suitcases full of Pinki's favourite things – home-made mango chutney, cauliflower pickle, chat-masala, papadum, Indian frying pans, silk saris – and everything else Pinki had requested. Pinki said, 'Sister, for a few days you're going to take it easy here, have fun going around and seeing the city. There's no need to start looking for work right away.'

Guddo was a first-rate cook. Every day she would take pains to prepare some special dish to delight Pinki and Satinder when they came home in the evening, tired out from their jobs. They had completely forgotten what it was like in the old days in India when there was always someone to see to these things.

The house was still crowded but at least it was not so bad as before. There was a difference of six years between Raju and Arjun, so there were not many occasions when the two of them would squabble. Like Arjun, Raju was enrolled in a state school nearby, not one of the best but a private school was far beyond the resources of both sisters for the moment.

For the next two months Guddo stayed at home, cooking and looking after Pinki's apartment. Jijaji, who still resented the way Pinki had accepted his departure without coaxing him to stay, said one day, 'Pinki's found herself a servant she doesn't have to pay – now Guddo won't have to look for any other job.'

Guddo was annoyed, even though she knew Jijaji's sarcasm came from his having had such a bad time himself, but it wasn't her fault that she hadn't found a job. Every day Pinki would instruct her to find out about such and such a place or phone another or send out an application. But somehow or other there was never a sign of any kind of job in sight. Even before the question of teaching arose Guddo had been told that she wasn't sufficiently qualified and she herself would have to do further study. 'Further study,' meant college fees, so for the moment it was out of the question.

An acquaintance of Pinki's, who had just set up a news stall on a subway station platform a few blocks away from the apartment, told Guddo he had a job for her if she wanted it. The pay was a bit above the minimum wage set by law, and there was also the possibility of overtime. The news stall was open from seven in the morning until one a.m. Guddo felt that it was demeaning for the widow of a prominent engineer to sell newspapers, but at this point she was completely out of money and even had to ask Pinki for carfare to get around in the city. So she started working.

Standing in a small square space walled with thick plastic, surrounded by rows of newspapers, magazines, cigarettes, chocolate and candy, Guddo felt as though she herself were stuffed into a pack of cigarettes. The door behind her remained closed all the time; in front of her was a rectangular window through which she handed out the newspapers and candies to customers and took in the money. Through the transparent plastic sheet fronting the stall Guddo watched the steady flow of passers-by on the station platform. From eight o'clock on, young and old alike would come rushing down the stairs on the way to their offices. As soon as a train stopped each brilliantly lit car would fill with the crowd of passengers, jammed tight together, with coats and scarves sometimes snared in the automatic doors. Guddo was reminded of her college days; conditions on the New York trains, she thought, were no better. Around ten o'clock the rush diminished, office workers giving way to elderly people, mothers with babies in strollers, or school children with their teachers on an outing.

Prakash Patel, the owner of the stall, was a shrewd businessman and had established several other similar news stands. He would often make a surprise visit to check up on the intake of cash. Guddo had a green card but most of his employees were

11

illegal Indian immigrants who had no work permit so he could pay them salaries below the minimum wage.

The work was hard for Guddo. Her legs and feet hurt from standing for so many hours behind the counter, and she suffered because she was afraid to use the ladies' room after Pinki and Satinder had told her so many frightening stories of the murders and muggings that took place there. She was fearful, too, just to be on the subway platform, for as soon as a train left, a sinister silence fell upon the station. Only the sound of someone's footsteps on the stairs would relieve her anxiety. But when she told Patel about her fears he surprised her by showing no concern. 'You have your job, do it or be on your way – there's no shortage of people looking for work here, you know.' Guddo was accustomed to polite and considerate treatment from Indian men. Patel, though not positively rude, was blunt and bossy, all the while he kept her at a distance. She was furious with him – men like him used to be lucky if her husband gave them jobs as clerks in his office – who did he think he was? Anyway, she couldn't stay stuck in this job forever, she'd have to talk to Pinki right away.

Because the station was underground Guddo was also much troubled by the cold. Her shoulders had even begun to ache from the weight of the heavy coat she had to wear all the time. She must simply try to find a job in some fashion boutique, she told herself, she'd had enough of Patel and his news stall.

Four

'Are you from Pakistan?'

The questioner was an elderly American, staring at her through the news stall window. He had been standing there for some time, turning over the pages of *Playboy*. When she looked up and saw him, the magazine was opened to a picture of a naked girl. Embarrassed, Guddo hesitated to answer him. Then, turning away, she said casually, 'No, from India.'

'I was there, you know, during the war, in Calcutta,' he said in Hindi. 'How do you like it here?'

Guddo was happy to hear her own language from an American. They went on talking and in no time at all she felt they were old friends. In the coming days he would often stop by her stall to ask how she was. If she was busy with customers he would hang back until they were gone. One day he asked her, 'You're very beautiful, you know, you're well educated too – how can you do work like this?'

Guddo merely smiled a faint smile.

The old gentleman was retired and lived alone. His wife had died three years before, his son and daughter had settled in California and rarely came to visit him, so his was a lonely life, wandering about, shopping, tending to insignificant matters.

At first Guddo listened to his stories with some enjoyment, but very soon she found that he repeated himself endlessly, and she lost interest in him. When he showed up she would busy herself doing the accounts or giving change. While she worked she saw only the customers' impatient hands, for by the time she gave them their change and raised her eyes their faces had already disappeared; the old man's was the only face she recognised, so she remained just as alone as he on the other side of the news stall plastic.

The train was just pulling out. Again the dreadful silence took possession of the station platform. An occasional sound of footsteps sometimes reassured Guddo, sometimes frightened her even more. Hearing a sudden movement she raised her eyes towards the window and found herself staring straight into the barrel of a gun. A tall black man was holding a pistol steady on her; she heard him say, 'Put all your cash through the window, be quick about it!'

Completely numb, Guddo automatically opened the cash drawer, took out whatever money was there, and passed it through the window.

The man quickly stuffed his pockets and like a flash was already on his way up the stairs. At this moment there were still a few people on the platform but they were all watching the tracks, they seemed to have noticed nothing at all. Stunned, Guddo could not even cry out. All she could think was, What if he had killed me? Customers began to appear again. No one said anything. Guddo's whole body was trembling. Handing out the change once more, she kept seeing that pistol in every hand. She felt she couldn't stay another minute in the stall; without hesitating another second, she locked it up and ran home to pour out her terror to Pinki.

'I almost got killed today,' she said, sobbing.

'What are you talking about?'

'I don't know what God is trying to do to me! Has He ever shown me any kindness?'

'For heaven's sake, tell me what happened!'

'Believe me, I'm never going to work in that stall again.'

After she heard the story, Pinki immediately called Patel. When he heard what had happened he said, 'Have the police been informed?'

'My sister came running home right after it happened, and I thought I ought to call you first.'

'You should have called the police immediately! By now there won't be any witnesses to the robbery.'

And in fact, there hadn't been any witness – confirming Patel's suspicion that Guddo might have stolen the money herself. So she lost her job and a whole week's salary as well. A report was lodged with the police, but nothing came of it. Pinki told her, 'Robberies like this go on every day here. If somebody gets killed then these people will make an investigation, but no one's concerned with small-scale muggings like this. And as for the wages Patel owes you, forget it! If you sued him the lawyers would cost more than what you'd get from him. So that's it, just put it behind you and look for some other kind of work.'

That night the hand holding the pistol swam constantly before Guddo's eyes. With trembling lips she began to repeat a prayer in Sanskrit: ' "Oh Lord, take our sorrow away." Why can't things happen the way we want? Please, please grant us what we ask! . . .'

Five

In only a month Guddo found another job, this time far from the apartment, as a salesgirl in a store where they sold fancy kitchen goods and household wares. The atmosphere here, at least, was better. As she looked around Guddo thought that when she had her own place she would buy just this size of bottle or tin for her spices, there would be the same kind of garlands of onions and baskets of potatoes hanging, the same enamelled pots. Until she had seen them she had never imagined a kitchen could be so beautiful.

Around the time she began her new job, things at home began to change. When she first arrived Guddo took responsibility for all the housework to relieve Pinki of the burden. Even after she started full-time work, Guddo remained responsible for it. Falling into the routine of her job, she now began to find it burdensome to do the cooking and household chores. It occurred to her that what Jijaji had said – about Pinki having a servant for nothing – was true. Guddo wondered why her sister couldn't see that she too got home from work worn out. So now she began to let the housework go. She would give Raju some money to buy himself a slice of pizza, while she herself grabbed a bite to eat at work or else brought a sandwich with her. When for two days running she deliberately came home late she found Pinki already busy cooking dinner. The third day Guddo got back at her usual time but stayed out of the kitchen, putting on a show of helping Raju with his schoolwork instead. Pinki waited until half-past ten for Guddo to come into the kitchen before she made the dinner.

Pretty soon this violation of the established domestic order began to cause trouble.

'There's not one clean undershirt!' Satinder shouted at Pinki. 'The bathroom's piled high with dirty clothes.'

Shocked, Pinki shrilled back, 'There's so much work, how much do you expect me to do alone?'

She put a lot of emphasis on that 'alone'. Guddo was no fool; she had been aware for some time that her sister was exploiting her. Pinki was the younger, after all, and still when she came to visit in India Guddo wouldn't let her so much as wash a dish – why couldn't she do the same for her?

By now Pinki was beginning to feel the pinch of supporting Guddo. It occurred to her that since Guddo had had a steady job for quite a few months she ought to start looking for her own place to live. As soon as Gita and Jijaji had found work they took it upon themselves to leave. But Guddo, despite Pinki's not too subtle hints, never so much as mentioned moving to a separate apartment. Surely she'd saved enough money by now, Pinki brooded, so why did she keep hanging around? Maybe Biji was right – Guddo took from everybody so long as her victim didn't get fed up and stop giving. Her sign was Scorpio, and remember what they say – those born under Scorpio take advantage of other people, then cast them off like a fly out of the milk.

Gita was not slow to give her opinion. 'She may be a widow, but is there anything she has to go without? Her kids eat and dress better than we do, and they study in the best schools, what else can she ask for? And just look, neither of us owns a house but Guddo has one in India, doesn't she? She was saving up the money she took from us way back then so she could have that house built. By getting everyone to sympathise with her because she's a widow she finds somebody to do her work and somebody else to send her the tickets. By weeping and wringing her hands in front of Jijaji she got him to pay her monthly expenses, and now she doesn't even remember it.'

Satinder's tolerance also began to wear thin. One day he said to Pinki, 'Why should I keep putting up with your family? We've done enough. Now that she has a decent job why doesn't she find

17

her own place? You know Toni wants to come so we're going to have to make some arrangement for him.'

Toni was Satinder's younger brother, who was planning to come to New York in a couple of months to study.

That same day Satinder, in a rage, struck Raju. He never had liked the boy's attitude. He told Pinki, 'Your sister's completely spoiled the brat. He's not going to survive here, I tell you. The kids in this country see to their own meals, but he can't even lift a finger. Doesn't Arjun make his own snacks when he comes home from school? But Raju has to wait until his mother or one of us waits on him.'

And to Raju he said, 'Your mother's turned you into a sissy. If you keep on like this over here you're never going to get anywhere at all.'

No one understood just what was happening to Raju. His naturally lively temperament was imprisoned within the dingy walls of the apartment. Sometimes when he was sitting, completely silent, he would suddenly go into a rage over nothing at all and start yelling. Once, coming back from school, a gang of boys beat him up for no reason. Raju was hurt psychologically as much as physically, and the fear grew up in him that it wasn't safe to play outside. His surroundings seemed utterly baffling to him, quite beyond his control. He had entered a strange and alien world.

Arjun, six years younger than Raju, had his own group of friends. Though he held the status of elder brother, Raju at twelve still felt the need to play with other children. The change from the comfortable life in Chandigarh frightened him. He didn't want to trouble his mother with complaints – and in any case, he didn't have the sort of complaint he could express in plain words. From home to school, from school straight back home, then the homework, television, or reading comics – such was his whole routine.

One day when Arjun called him a sissy, he lost his temper and struck him. When she heard Arjun crying, Pinki's pent-up anger

18

exploded; she slapped Raju several times and said, 'Since you people came there's been no peace in this house! Every minute you're causing trouble.' Although this stung Raju more than anything, he didn't complain to his mother even now, but simply said, 'Mummy, I think the house and school in Chandigarh were a lot better.'

Guddo began to realise that they couldn't stay with Pinki much longer. But it was going to be difficult to find a decent place to live on her salesgirl's salary. She wanted to put off moving for a little while at least, but then Raju said, 'Mummy, you told me we'd get rich when we went to America but now we're here we're poorer than ever, and Uncle's angry and Arjun thinks he's better than us – I don't understand what's going on here.'

There was no possibility of returning to India. She wouldn't be able to pay the five thousand rupees for Tanima's medical school out of a teacher's salary. However badly things were going here in New York, she was still rich in terms of Indian rupees. And she could earn a little extra by working overtime. Guddo stiffened her resolve. She would stay, even if it meant more squabbling. She now began to do the grocery shopping to lighten Pinki's burden. And she became ever more careful about spending anything – and still, when you counted it in rupees how much she had to spend every day just for carfare! She was only earning three dollars an hour. If she worked in a fashion boutique then she'd have to have better clothes to wear on the job. At first she borrowed Pinki's skirts and blouses, even though she felt strangely ashamed when she wore them. But at her new job she had to wear a suitable uniform when she was behind the counter. It was all right to wear saris or *salwar-qamiz* at home, and she had lots of fine embroidered saris still packed in cases which would be taken out only for parties and other special occasions. For his part, Raju needed warm jackets and all sorts of other clothes. So any idea of a new place to live had to be postponed. Just the same, she had a look at a few apartments, but for one reason or another all of them were unacceptable. And the rents were so high that when she heard them she was stunned into silence.

Six

The next time Guddo got her pay cheque she went out during her lunch break, cashed it, and bought some games for Raju and playthings for Arjun. On the way home that evening, though she was tired from all her running around at lunchtime, she still felt light-hearted, thinking that Arjun would be pleased with his toys and this might relieve the tense atmosphere in the apartment.

But when she came through the front door of the apartment house and started up the stairs she was struck with a presentiment of something wrong. Brushing it aside, she hurried straight on to the apartment, put the key in the lock and opened the door. She was still thinking of the packages in her hand until she looked inside and was scarcely able to believe the sight that met her eyes. Her big trunk was lying on the floor not far from the door, and close by, Raju sat on a stool staring at it; he looked terrified. Her clothes were scattered all about as though they had been pulled from their hangers and thrown down in anger. Before she could grasp what had happened, Pinki came rushing from the kitchen, shouting:

'Please, sister, have mercy on us, let me live in peace! We have our lives too, you know. I can't stand any more of this! Quarrelling every day, Satinder in a rage – I can't take it!' Then softening her angry tone a little, she went on, 'I'm sorry I have to be so rude but you've really gone too far. You've been earning a living for a long time now, so please, can't you make some other arrangements for yourself?'

Guddo was speechless. In her wildest dreams she had never imagined a scene like this. Today the pistol was in her sister's hand; she felt the panic shoot through her like a bullet. All she could manage to say, in a weak voice, was 'What . . . what happened?'

And now Satinder was confronting her, his words striking her ears like hammer blows. 'We spent our hard-earned money to bring her here and she doesn't give a damn about us. If I ask Raju to go to the store to bring me a bottle of soda he doesn't even get off the bed. I ask you, is there any reason we have to run ourselves ragged waiting on her? Do we even have to go out and find her a place to live too? Tell her, it doesn't matter where she goes but she can't stay here. I won't have them in the house a minute longer!'

Guddo stood there, as though stupefied. She had no idea where she could go at this time of night. Softly she said, 'Look, Pinki, don't put us out on the street. Starting tomorrow I'll look for another place. Whatever kind of place I find, I'll move. But where can I go at this hour?'

The only person she knew in the neighbourhood was the old gentleman who spoke Hindi. If she'd taken a liking to him he could have been useful at a moment like this – but she'd never bothered to find out his address or even his name.

With Satinder standing by, Pinki spoke even more angrily. 'You've been looking at other places for a long time but you always turn your nose up. When that Gujarati girl wanted to share her place with you why didn't you go? But the truth is, you'd have had to pay your full share then while you could live here for nothing . . .'

'But how could I share with anybody when I have Raju? And after seeing what sharing is here . . .'

This last sentence infuriated Pinki. All Guddo had meant was that in order to keep up her son's education and assure his independence she really ought to have her own place all to herself, but it came out in this sarcastic way. But Guddo was the one to be hurt as Pinki burst out:

'Yes, if only you knew how to share! Right from the beginning everybody told me that Indians didn't have any idea of how to live in a civilised way. You've made this apartment so dirty I

21

hate to step inside it. Everything's in disorder, everything out of place. You can't keep house the way you did in India, the standards here are rather different, you know!'

This attack struck at Guddo's whole sense of herself as a civilised person; no longer humble, she suddenly launched a counter attack. 'Oh marvellous, and I suppose you're an angel of cleanliness? Oh yes, you've turned into a real American. I suppose you were born here? I've seen your idea of cleanliness. Stuffing the dirty clothes under the beds, shutting up all the filth in closets and drawers and spraying fragrances, that's your idea of being clean. Don't think you're so high and mighty – you came from the same place I did! Just because you've got a few dollars now it's gone to your head, so you think you can simply throw me out of your house. Just where do you get off ordering me around? If my husband were alive today we'd see if you'd dare insult your big sister like this. I brought you up with my own hands, I washed your diapers, and you talk about being clean! You used to come back from the toilet smeared with filth, you didn't even know enough to keep your nose clean.'

Losing all control, she yelled, 'I spit, I *spit* on your house! God will punish you for the way you've treated me, don't think He won't! You can't put me out, I'm leaving. God brought me here, God will take care of me now. And to think I thought I should feel grateful to you! What right have you anyway to invite me or send me away? It's God alone who can do such things!'

Guddo's whole body felt as though it were on fire, her hands trembled with her emotion. Raju was frightened: he had never before seen his mother act like this. Throwing his arms around her he shouted, 'Stop it, Mummy, please stop it!' Then, in a frightened voice, 'Can't we go to Aunt Gita's house, Mummy?'

At this Guddo, suddenly aware of her helplessness, burst into tears. 'My fate is cursed,' she said. 'Otherwise would we ever have come here? We're going to have to go wandering the streets, that's what it's come to. If they meant to treat us so badly why did they send for us? Now they call us dirty and stingy! But when they came to our house they stayed for months at a time. How cruel they are, how unjust! Only God can punish them for it.'

As she said this Guddo felt like some pure spirit whose curse is all-powerful. Pinki and Satinder stood there in silence. Though they regretted what had happened and felt it was their duty to persuade her not to leave they couldn't get out the words that might stop her. They feared that if they said anything at all she might actually stay and start up the trouble all over again. Because the best thing for everybody – no one could doubt it! – would be for Guddo to go away. They stood silent, waiting for her to take her first step out through the door.

Seven

In the taxi on the way to Gita's house Guddo tried to calm herself by reciting *mantras*, the *mantras* for the fire sacrifice which she had memorised. '*Yatkamaste* . . .' What could that sage have meant by desire? All Vedic philosophy, all the *mantras* always spoke of bringing happiness to this earthly life, even the happiness of material success as well . . . For through performing all those actions and all those rituals, one reaches the Supreme Being. But was self-realisation really the truth of life? For self-realisation was a kind of selfishness. Pettiness and weakness too . . .

So what must I do? Guddo wondered. Was she doing the right thing now? At this point she couldn't retreat to India, she'd get nowhere at all with a teacher's salary of 700 rupees. No, she had to go on here, this was where she was fated to struggle.

Gita had settled in Flushing, about twenty kilometres away, where housing was much cheaper than in Manhattan. A lot of Indians who came to New York had taken up residence in Flushing. Shops selling Indian saris, Indian groceries and appliances running on 220 volts – destined to be sent back home – were becoming more numerous as more and more Indians came here to live.

Gita's apartment was on the seventh floor of a ten-storey building that had an elevator. With only two bedrooms the apartment offered no room to spare. Gita's three children, Kanika, Radhika and Ashok, slept in one of the bedrooms, Gita and Jijaji in the other, so they arranged for Guddo and Raju to sleep in the living room. Every night a mattress and bedding were put down on the floor, and early every morning Guddo would go off to work, Raju to school, and the room became a living room again. By day there was no one at home to use it except Jijaji, whose work hours were from either four in the afternoon to midnight or midnight to eight in the morning. Daytime was when he got most of his sleep. When Ashok and Radhika came back from school around three-thirty they sometimes saw Jijaji for a few minutes, as a matter of duty, and often did not see him at all. Radhika was thirteen now, Ashok eleven, and Kanika, who at sixteen was in her last year of high school, did not come home until around five-thirty.

Every morning and every evening the apartment was terribly crowded and full of noisy bickering. Among the children there was never an end to the disputes over which TV programme to watch. Radhika, sharp-tongued when she was angry, would trade insults in English with Ashok. All evening the telephone kept ringing, mostly calls from Radhika's girlfriends, and she would talk for hours. Though they scolded her constantly, she just kept on doing what she wanted.

Kanika's position in the household was somewhat different: her parents took everything she said very seriously. Gita often remarked on how intelligent Kanika was, and Kanika, as though aware of her importance, did not talk much with anyone at home. Every evening she had to see to some serious work for school, term papers and the like, and as soon as she got back would shut herself up in her parents' room to study.

It took Guddo an hour and a half to get home from work by subway every evening, and she worried constantly about Raju, who also had a long subway ride to school. One day she'd seen three boys get up from the seat across the aisle, pull out revolvers, and order all the passengers to hand over their money and jewelry. When one man took too much time one of the boys fired at him and he collapsed. Guddo could not tell if he was wounded or dead. She had to give them her gold chain, her watch and the few dollars she was carrying. The moment the train stopped the three boys ran off with their bag of loot. There was a commotion and the train was held in the station for a long time while the police took away the man who'd been shot and questioned the passengers.

Guddo experienced less panic in this shared experience than she had when she was robbed earlier, but her general uneasiness increased. Here anything could happen at any time! Would the man who'd been shot survive? Her mouth felt as dry as cotton wool from anxiety. Her Raju . . . he too was constantly riding the trains. And those boys looked no older than high school students. She would have to ask the principal not to keep Raju late at school, he had to be home by four. She really must have him transfer to a school closer to home. Every day now she kept giving him special instructions. Often she would meet him near the store and the two would come back together. As soon as she stepped into one of the trains, that scene always rose before her eyes and she would silently recite *mantras* for Raju's safety and her own. She consoled herself by thinking that whenever you did anything at all – even just getting into the train – if you remembered a *mantra*, your wishes would be fulfilled. This was the best she could do to quiet her anxiety.

Right from the beginning Gita made it clear that Guddo was expected to contribute to the household expenses. Everything was so expensive that she and Jijaji already used their full salary to keep up and could not get by supporting two more people. So Guddo was to give her three hundred dollars every month – Guddo whose monthly salary was a mere six hundred. But this way, at least, she wasn't obliged to feel beholden to anybody. Still, she was shocked that her sister wanted to make money at her expense. But this could only be Jijaji's idea – since he was unsuccessful in every other undertaking, he could at least make money through her. Well, Guddo, for her part, had managed to save up some money while she was staying at Pinki's – one had to make the most of every opportunity.

And Jijaji, poor fellow, how could he be happy working as a doorman? It was no better than being a *chaprasi* or a *peon* in India. And perhaps he had suffered even more than Guddo. He was still selling at the sidewalk market on the weekends. So every Saturday and Sunday it was a ritual for the whole family to pick up the goods, bring them to the sidewalk to spread out, pack up what was left, and finally count the money they had made. But they never made very much. Brass ashtrays and candlesticks, Nataraj figures and the rest of it had all become very commonplace by now. Jijaji said, 'When this stuff that's left over is finished we won't buy any new goods. Why keep on doing something you find unpleasant?' But didn't he find working as a doorman unpleasant too? Well, at least he earned a living from it. On the surface he looked very much the same but his words revealed his inner dissatisfaction and hostility. Because of his insecurity a strange kind of miserliness had affected his way of doing business – he kept an account of every penny and would spend nothing without long and careful consideration. Above and beyond the household expenses there was the cost of the children's education. If Kanika had not won a scholarship her school fees would have taken his whole salary and Gita's too. While she studied, Kanika also earned a bit by working a few hours in a library. Guddo felt that Jijaji's attitude and behaviour had changed very much, or perhaps until now she had never really known him.

One day she said to him, 'I've heard that almonds and pistachios are very cheap near the place where you work. When there's somebody going to India I'd like to send along some for my daughters. Do you think you could bring me six or seven pounds?'

She had hardly finished speaking when Jijaji answered, 'Give me the money for it in advance, and a couple of dollars for the subway fare both ways.'

Years before, when Guddo's husband died and she wanted to sell the twin beds, this same Jijaji had immediately taken out five hundred rupees and said, 'Take this, but don't sell the beds, they'll be something to remember Premkumarji by.' What had happened to that generosity of his since then? Now it seemed as though he was caressing every dollar with his eyes.

Guddo, feeling like an unwanted paying guest, was more and more uncomfortable in Gita's apartment. It wasn't convenient for Raju to study either; he had no quiet little corner to himself.

Guddo reflected, I'm paying three hundred every month and still it isn't the least bit like having my own home. So she began again to look for her own place and after some time found a one-room basement apartment for rent in a five-storey building not far from Gita's. The rent was a hundred and seventy-five dollars a month. Even though it was dark and damp in the basement, Guddo felt an intense need for privacy and peace, and Raju too had been waiting so long for the same thing. When Gita found out, she was aghast. She felt that Guddo had betrayed her by finding a new place on the sly, while Jijaji was angry at the extra income he was going to lose if Guddo left. Furthermore, he would miss teasing and flirting with her, for this had become a habit with him.

For her part, Guddo was now fed up with his amorous advances. He liked to put his hand on her shoulder and at night he'd ask her why she was arranging her bedding on the living room floor when she could come and sleep in his bed. Guddo always responded to his flirting with harsh reproaches. If Jijaji had been able somehow to console himself that Guddo was attracted to him, of course she would have been even more welcome in the house. But from the beginning Guddo had never given the slightest indication that she liked him at all. She had always been something of a puzzle to Jijaji. One evening after Premkumar's death, when they were both alone in the house in Chandigarh, he insisted that she come and see a film with him. She had refused, saying that if people saw them going out together, God knew what they would make of it. But now there were no people to see, and Guddo was tired to death of his constant jokes about 'Sister-in-law is half a wife,' and the like.

Guddo had never found Jijaji attractive; now that he had come down in the world she positively disliked him. She was one of those women for whom a man's worth depended not so much on his personal qualities as upon his social and financial status. When she became a widow her grief stemmed mostly from her realisation that she would no longer be regarded as the wife of an important official. That was why she spent beyond her capacity, to make sure her children received a superior education so that

28

they too could attain some status. And where she herself was concerned, she wanted to go on studying chiefly as a means of earning a better salary. For when her daughters came to New York they would not be able to get along on her salesgirl's wages.

She was determined to find something better. Then she learned that the federal government had established a job-training programme in Chinatown for poor people, citizens and immigrants alike. It included a course in accounting which offered a scholarship of one hundred dollars a week. With her MA in English, Guddo was more than qualified for acceptance. The only drawback was that even though she had been the wife of an officer of high rank her name would have to be listed among the city's poor and needy. So she looked around a bit more, but when nothing came through she went ahead and applied for the Federal training programme.

Eight

Guddo kept searching for another place, but there wasn't another one-room apartment to be found for under four hundred dollars, so finally she and Raju moved into the basement flat. At this moment Guddo needed, more than anything else, a place of her own where she and Raju might live in peace. Though it was depressing, the basement offered her a welcome refuge.

There was no trouble in finding furniture. She bought new beds, the rest she got second-hand, or for nothing at all off the trash piles. She had even found a quite decent table and chairs and a sofa discarded out on the street. So, whatever else, they were getting by.

At this point Guddo began to worry about her daughters. The elder was now doing her MSc and would have to begin a PhD programme when she came. Guddo was uneasy too about leaving the girls in a boarding school. She would often wake in the middle of the night and start fretting as she realised that everything now depended on her own inner strength and nothing else.

The desire for independence which had driven Guddo to the new apartment was gradually turning into a feeling of intense loneliness. In her sisters' homes there might be endless quarrelling, but there was a warm feeling of security too. Now she was constantly tormented by anxiety. If something happened to her or to Raju, how would the other manage to get by alone?

One Sunday she was so depressed that she began crying and couldn't stop. She couldn't do any work, she couldn't read. Raju was away on a school trip for the weekend. She wished she could call her daughters but knew that would cost the earth. For solace she telephoned Gita.

'Did you know,' Gita said, 'today is Krishna Janmashtami. I'm just getting ready to go to the temple.'

'And I'm just sitting around doing nothing,' said Guddo. 'But where is this temple?'

'I know – just come along with me!'

Nine

Guddo found some consolation in going to the temple that day.
She thought she would make a habit of going every Sunday, but
still a lot of Sundays went by without her returning. After
enduring the deafening racket of the subway train five days a
week she simply didn't feel she could go through it all over again
on her day off. The subway roar, ripping through the early
morning, changed the silence within the earth into another roar.

Guddo had now become a part of the bustle and confusion she
used to observe while she was standing behind the counter of the
news stand. Now she too would push people out of her way in
her haste to arrive at work on time. At such times people would
complain: 'Don't push!' 'Stop shoving!' and sometimes even:
'Please don't push,' but like the others Guddo paid no heed.

People of so many different races and colours had come to live
in New York that Guddo, glancing around the subway car,
thought she could identify as many as a dozen different nation-
alities at a time. Distinguishing among them by their dress was
difficult as they mostly dressed in the American way: the
difference was in the style. Some wore fashionable suits and ties,
others patched jeans. But it didn't necessarily follow that somebody wearing patched jeans was any less wealthy than the others.
Some of the girls wore make-up so thick they looked as though
they were wearing masks, while others were so indifferent and
careless that their hair was positively dishevelled. Guddo had
never before seen such startling contrasts of races and styles all
together in one place. When people saw her dressed in the

American way they often assumed she was Hispanic and a man once addressed her in Spanish.

That Sunday when she went to the temple, Raju had been away on a school trip. When she was ringing the temple bells her hand hit against someone else's hand. She heard a man say, 'Excuse me!' in a voice that sounded vaguely familiar, perhaps because of the Panjabi accent; and when her eyes met his she found his face familiar too, reminding her of home. Unable to suppress her pleasure in this recognition, she asked him, 'Do you live in New York, or are you just on a visit from India?'

'No, I live here.'

And so the conversation began. His name was Juneja, he was a doctor, director of paediatrics in a hospital. His wife was also a doctor, they had two children, and his mother lived with them. They had all come to the temple that day. It turned out that the doctor's mother was acquainted with Guddo's; the family came from the same district and they also used to meet at the Arya Samaj temple in Delhi. She told Guddo that they rarely came to this South Indian temple. There was a North Indian 'Gita' temple which Gujaratis attended; she herself usually went to the New York Arya Samaj temple. When they set out for home they dropped Guddo off at her apartment. Dr Juneja gave her his card and wrote down Guddo's telephone number on another card.

This was the very first time that Guddo had met a person with whom a bond of spontaneous friendship might be formed: a natural attraction, no formality in their conversation, as though they had become acquainted long before. Guddo felt hapy as she rarely had since coming to New York.

But afterwards – a long silence. When Guddo telephoned his house once or twice Mrs Juneja picked up the phone; from her voice it was clear she was not terribly pleased to hear from Guddo. A formal exchange of generalities, and nothing more. Guddo sensed that she had not hit it off with Juneja, after all.

In the days following she was lost once more in her daily routine. She had now begun to study accounting. This meant

33

being in school from nine in the morning until five in the afternoon; after that, homework, dinner, housework and the like.

It wasn't easy to start studying all over again at the age of forty-five; and she was used to an Indian educational system. After Premkumar died it had not been difficult to go on and get her BT and MA. But accounting was an entirely new subject for her and she had to struggle with it. Still, after her husband's death there had been born in her an instinct for survival like some wild animal's, which no matter how many beatings it suffered would spring up to do battle again and again. Often she would weep over her helplessness and curse her fate along with her relatives; but then she was ready to begin fighting all over again. She had been alone in her struggle in India and she was even more alone here. In India when she was in trouble she could count on some help from her husband's friends and from her own brothers and sisters. But here even her sisters had become strangers.

She thought back on how the lawyer Batra, her neighbour, had taken care of all the paperwork for getting her pension and provident fund. He had not tried to make her feel grateful but, on the contrary, told her that he thought himself fortunate that she considered him worthy of serving her.

Mrs Batra had been angry with her husband. 'Just look, there you are spending all your time doing favours for Guddo Chaddha!' Once she had even said in Guddo's hearing, 'I've been telling you all month that the roof's leaking and you absolutely must call somebody in to fix it. But you'll do that only when you find a free moment from the work you're doing for other people!'

What could Guddo say? She had already heard this sort of thing many times before. Now she wasn't going to worry about it, and anyway, why should she? She needed Mr Batra's help time and time again. She realised that he was attracted to her and she was determined to take as much advantage of it as possible. And the lawyer himself used to say, 'Please, Mrs Chaddha, when you go to America don't forget all about us! If you want, I'll come too and help you all I can. You will ask me to come, won't you?'

Guddo laughed when he talked like that and thought no more about it. At that time it was not even certain that she would emigrate to America. But when it seemed probable that she would go abroad, his suggestion took on a particular significance. Even Mrs Batra came to tolerate her then. After Guddo came to America her daughters might even go to stay with the Batras when they were on holiday.

In those days when she was having the house built, it was Batra who saw to the licence, the gas, the permit for the cement, and all the other things connected with the construction. And then he got his friend who was an IAS officer to recommend her for her school-teaching job. Guddo had kept the possibility of any physical involvement out of their relationship. Her strongly developed inhibitions would not let her acknowledge her desire. Her mother, brought up in the traditions of the Arya Samaj, had taught her daughters above all that the greatest success in life consisted in mastering the senses, telling them that this is what kept people under control and gave them honour. Fear that the daughters might stray on to some undesirable path dictated the conduct of every household. So from the beginning they kept themselves prepared for confronting some such inevitable catastrophe. Every Sunday while the *havan* was performed, prayers were offered for acquiring the strength to maintain control over desire, anger, intoxication and seduction, with a special solicitation to be saved from the mire of lust.

Biji used to say, 'Just see, these men are all very lustful. They want only one thing every day. If your father had his way he'd still have me making babies in my old age. We had seven, now two of them have died, but is that my fault? It ruined my health too. I couldn't begin to tell you how many illnesses this body of mine has suffered. You girls had better be careful about your health.'

Guddo had already had a couple of strange and frightening experiences which she felt unable to tell Biji about. They were very bad things, there was no telling what Biji would make of them. She was no longer sure how old she'd been, probably seven or eight. All the children were together playing hide-and-seek.

35

The father of one of her girlfriends was given the job of keeping one child's eyes covered and calling out after each of the others had found a place to hide. It was evening and the twilight dimness had already begun to invade the rear garden. When it was Guddo's turn she sat in the man's lap to have her eyes covered. Spreading one hand over her eyes, he thrust the other into her underpants. That hand was trying to find something there. Guddo wanted to get away but the weight of his hand pulled her back. Struggling again with all her strength, she managed to slip away. Suddenly the twilight seemed as terrifying to her as total darkness. She did not start searching for her hidden friends, she even forgot that they were playing a game. When she reached home she sat in silence on the doorstep for some time – that was all she remembered now.

Then something else happened one or two years later. Bullu, the neighbours' son, was playing with her in the swing. While they were swinging she became aware of a thick, soft pressure over her underpants. At once she thrust her foot out onto the ground, stopped the swing, and jumped off, yelling:

'I'm not going to play with you! You're dirty!'

And she was afraid that she might catch some disease.

When she began to have her period she at first suspected it was some kind of dangerous illness. Once or twice in the past when she had seen blood-stained rags in the bathroom, she thought her mother must have contracted a disease.

As she grew older she exercised every possible restraint over her feelings; even after her marriage this inclination did not change. She had observed that following only a few years of marriage her girlfriends were likely to complain of one illness or another. And they generally became stout and flabby. After she had married, Guddo herself, if she felt a pain in her side, would think that it came from an overindulgence in sensual pleasures. She would say to her husband, 'Leave me alone tonight. The same thing every day – you'll end up making me ill.'

Sometimes with caresses, sometimes with violence, her husband would manage to overcome her inhibitions. From him Guddo learned to enjoy a physical relationship. Little by little

36

her old repressions were melting away. When later on she herself came to express her desire, he would tease her. 'What in the world is happening to people? "I don't want to, it's dirty." Now? You Panjabi girls are just as hot as you're inhibited. Once the Bhakra Dam's opened what a flood there is.'

Once while caressing her legs he said, 'They say the hair on a girl's legs is connected with her sexual urge. So you must be full of it, the more I squeeze the more it springs up.'

After his death she once more completely suppressed those overflowing feelings, as though her spirit had been extinguished. Her psychological inhibitions and her fear of social disapproval had stopped the natural flow of her desire as though with walls of cement. Once when, as they were riding in his car, Batra had put his hand on her thigh, Guddo stopped him and said, 'Please, I don't like this at all.'

Batra answered, 'Very well, I won't touch you so long as you don't want it.' Despite what he'd said, occasionally his hand continued to stray here and there, to her thigh, to her shoulders and sliding from her shoulders down to her breasts.

At the time she was getting ready to come to America another disturbing thing happened. While she was sitting in a restaurant with Batra, chatting as they drank coffee, Batra was unable to control his desire to take Guddo in his arms. Guddo was furious and told him she was ready to break off their relationship forever. Batra sat there, restless, restraining himself with difficulty. Then he said with deliberation, 'Could you at least give me just one little hair from *there*?' Guddo felt as though a snake had sprung hissing from her body, but she sat there in silence. After that there was no chance of seeing Batra again, for the next day she had to set out for Delhi.

Guddo turned her thoughts back to the present. She was terribly worried because Raju had suddenly developed a fever, with a temperature of 103. She decided that somehow she must get in touch with Dr Juneja. Although his hospital was a considerable distance from her apartment she felt that she could be satisfied only by talking to him. She telephoned him and this

37

time he himself picked up the phone and said, 'Dr Juneja speaking.'

'Forgive me, I'm calling because I'm terribly worried, my son Raju . . .' At this point her voice gave way.

'Who? Is that Mrs Chaddha? What's the matter? I can't hear you any more.'

He recognised her voice. Even at this troubled moment her eyes began to sparkle. Just from hearing about Raju's condition on the phone, Dr Juneja prescribed some medicine. 'With a fever like that it's better not to have Raju come in. If this medicine doesn't bring his fever down, call me.'

When Raju was better, Guddo telephoned him again.

'Thanks very much. You were able to cure him over the phone.'

'Not at all, it wasn't difficult. He had all the symptoms of flu. So I didn't think it would be right to have him brought to the hospital. The flu takes its own time to be cured. You should get the credit for describing Raju's condition so accurately.'

'In that case, I should have been the doctor.'

'The doctor – or the patient?'

They both laughed.

'Fine, but now you must certainly come to our house sometime. Raju wants to meet his doctor too.'

'Certainly, just command and your faithful servant will oblige.'

But Guddo still hesitated to invite anyone to her apartment. She had all she could do to manage to stay there herself.

A few days later Dr Juneja telephoned. Guddo was pleased, realising that he had taken a liking to her. So she was still able to attract. And a man like Juneja, who had status, money, who could prove useful in a thousand ways, particularly to her daughter who was studying medicine – he could be a great help in advancing her in that direction.

Guddo's long-lost self-confidence was returning; since coming to New York, not one man, except for the old fellow in the subway, had let her know he found her attractive. Guddo thought that perhaps it was because she dressed in American clothes. She felt that skirts and slacks did not suit her figure. If she had not been afraid of her supervisor she would have worn only saris to her school. She knew that the sari suited her best of all. And Juneja, as it happened, had seen her in a sari that day at the temple, an emerald green Mysore chiffon. This colour flattered the golden glow of her naturally fair complexion and no doubt pleased him.

'Come next Saturday to dinner at my place,' he said.

'I'd like to, but alone at night . . .'

'Just come. Taking you home will be my responsibility.'

Juneja had bought a house far from the city in a rich neighbourhood encircled with trees and lawns. Guddo took a bus to get there; the doctor's son met her at the station and drove her to the house.

From the guests' conversation Guddo learned that the Junejas had only recently moved into this house from a smaller, more ordinary one. Mrs Juneja took a great deal of pleasure in showing Guddo and the other guests around the house. For Guddo everything there was a novelty. Sofas upholstered in contrasting burgundy velvet and light grey, which Guddo thought attractive. Animal figures of costly crystal on the glass tables among them, on the walls paintings in colours harmonising with the room, Spanish porcelain figurines on the shelves, tall palms ranged near the windows – everything astounded Guddo. It seemed as unreal to her as some fairyland. Here, then, was the country's fantasy of success made real!

Before all this alien splendour she felt diminished, pierced by the proud expression in Mrs Juneja's eyes. When the ceremony of viewing the house was over, Guddo came back into the living room and sank back on a sofa in one corner. The guests, forming small groups, clustered around the bar, drinking. The women formed a separate group, chatting about their latest acquisitions. Guddo had nothing of the sort to talk about: no house, no job. What was past was now a burden weighing her down as she crept along. The present had turned into a shameful situation. She was living only to see her children in the future settled in some kind of happy world just like this house, that alone was what she desired. *Yatkamaste! . . . vayam syama patayo rayinam . . .* The heaven of the future seemed more alluring than the heaven

39

of the past . . . they too would be masters of wealth and luxury. They too would have houses like palaces. For an instant all the guests vanished and Guddo saw Anima and Tanima, and the as yet unknown face of Raju's wife.

Juneja himself drove her home in his car; it was far away but he wouldn't hear of her going back alone so late at night.

'Did you enjoy the party?' In answer to this commonplace question Guddo suddenly poured out all the suffering, frustrations and resentments of her life. The time spent with her husband in splendid bungalows, her life alone after his death, coming to America – she went on describing it all. Only she still could not tell him about what it was like to live in a basement apartment.

Just as she had the other time, returning from the temple, now too Guddo wanted him to let her off at the corner before reaching the house, otherwise she would be obliged as a matter of courtesy to invite him into the apartment – and this was a risk she was not wiling to take. But Juneja would not listen to her.

'I must give you door-to-door service today,' he said. 'It's one a.m., how can I drop you at the corner?'

When the car stopped at her building, he kissed her lightly on the cheek and said, 'Hope to see you soon.'

A current of excitement ran through Guddo's whole body. After so many years she had felt the touch of a desirable man. For a moment she simply sat there, motionless.

As soon as she had recovered she began to try to open the door of the car. In her confusion she could not get hold of the handle. First the window would open, then when she grasped the handle she could not get it to move. Nervously she said, 'Every car in this country has a door that works differently.'

'It's all right, let me . . .'

Still sitting behind the wheel, he stretched his arm past Guddo toward the door. The upper part of his body seemed to stick to Guddo's, and she could smell the faint scent of his after-shave.

'There you are: it's open.' Feeling a little numb, Guddo murmured a thank you and stepped out. When he waved to her she waved back, then stood on the sidewalk until his car had disappeared.

Suddenly she realised that the street around her was completely deserted. The streetlights flickered silently; there was no sound but the distant hum of cars from the highway. Not wanting to waken Raju, she did not ring the bell. When she found her key and went inside she saw him still seated before the television, half-asleep. As soon as she entered the room he got up and, embracing her, asked her why she was so late.

He could not conceal from Guddo the uneasiness and concern in his complaint. She felt bad about it; she had never before left him alone so late at night. He must have been terribly afraid. Because he was already twelve she had not thought it necessary to get a babysitter, which in any case she couldn't afford.

Suddenly she felt as though yet another restriction had been put upon her – her life did not belong to her alone. She was abruptly jolted out of her fantasies about Juneja. Only think – putting Raju in danger just to go to a party! What if something had happened? She would never do anything like this again. Why hadn't she brought him along with her? Though Juneja hadn't invited him she could at least have asked. As it happened, Raju had no friend to play with at home, where there was nothing to do but study and watch television. And the television was old too, on its last legs, something the neighbours had thrown away, so the picture wasn't clear. Raju wasn't being brought up at all like a normal child. No place nearby to play, and a home that wasn't really like a home. Back in Chandigarh, as soon as he came into the house he would throw down his books and run out to play with his friends, he didn't even want to take time to have a snack. Here, as soon as he came home, he would turn on the television and, while it was on, sit in front of it and do his homework. At other times, he would be longing to play ball. He would throw the ball up toward the ceiling or at the walls. Once when the ball hit the bulb and the fragments of glass were scattered on the floor, Guddo was furious and said, 'No more ball playing inside, you'll have to go outside to play.'

But where was there to go outside? Even this bit of fun was denied to Raju.

So he went on constructing his peculiar private world. Television and books – these were his two companions. As for Guddo herself, what with school, shopping and housework, she could give him very little time. When he was in the mood, Raju would sometimes share in the housework. Often when Guddo was tired and felt depressed, he would make tea for her – but with a teabag. Without tea brewed every morning in the teapot she could not start any work; it was an addiction going back years. But here fresh-brewed tea was not the custom. Hot water and a teabag, and with lemon at that – could you even call it tea?

Guddo did not sleep well all through that night. She kept remembering home. Home, which wasn't anywhere now. Her daughters in the hostel, Raju in his private world, her husband in some other world, and the house rented out.

A letter had come from Tanima, telling her the tenants had not paid their rent for the last two months so she had not yet paid her college fees. Tanima asked her to send a money order or write to the tenants. Anima had come to see her last Sunday. She had borrowed some money from Mr Batra.

As she got to the end of the letter Guddo became aware of the hints of sadness in it. 'Mummy, medical study takes up the whole day from morning until evening, but as soon as I get some free time I think a lot about you and Raju. I'm glad when Anima or Uncle or Mr Batra come to visit. Mummy, I'd really like to come to stay with you. It's going to take another three years to finish my medical courses, so couldn't I come once in between to visit you? You could send me my ticket. I could come with Anima . . .'

Guddo felt overwhelmed with longing for her daughters. Her thoughts began to run far ahead. Next summer when she finished her accounting courses she could have Tanima come over.

The next day was Sunday. Because she hadn't slept well she felt somewhat enervated all day. On Sundays she usually did the laundry in the coin-operated washing machines in the building across the street. With a great effort, she gathered up the clothes in a basket and, after putting them in the machines, waited there in the basement for them to get washed, sitting for forty-five minutes with her hands folded, thinking and remembering. About her daughters, about Raju and Juneja. When she returned

42

home a couple of hours later after drying the clothes in the driers, she found Raju watching television again. Annoyed, she set the clothes down on the bed, ready to turn off the TV, but suddenly changed her mind. For what could she give Raju to compensate for the TV? For her part, she had washed the clothes and now, at home again, she would drink some tea and cook dinner. But apart from TV there was nothing else for Raju to do. The only games he could play were TV games, and he played them over and over again, trying to get ever higher scores. When he got the highest score possible for a particular game he wouldn't play it again. Then he'd say, 'Mummy, I'm bored with this game. There's a new game now, Donkey Kong. The TV ad looks interesting – will you get it for me?' And Guddo, considering her own needs less important, would give him whatever he asked for.

'Mummy,' he said, 'I forgot to tell you: Dr Juneja telephoned.'

'Now just see! You're so caught up in your TV you forgot to give me an important message.'

'But there wasn't any special message.'

'But still – didn't he say anything?'

'Only to call him when you got back.'

'Very good,' said Guddo, trying to control the wave of joy that swept over her. She wouldn't call him back just now but wait and see if he was going to call her again.

She did not have to wait long. After only an hour Juneja called again.

'You left your scarf in the car last night,' he said. 'So now I'll have to bring it to you, unless you come here.'

Much as she wanted to see him again, she did not want to quite so quickly.

'It really doesn't matter,' she said. 'I can pick it up whenever we happen to meet again.'

'Whatever you like. But just say the word and I'll bring it.'

'No, thanks, there's no need to bother.'

'All right, as you wish.' In Juneja's voice she picked up a hint of disappointment. And this, she thought, was fine.

Ten

It was Gita on the telephone.

'Next week's *Divali*. We all have a day off on Saturday, so I thought we might celebrate together. I've asked a few friends along with you and Pinki. Everyone's going to cook one dish to bring.'

'Then of course I'll bring something too,' said Guddo. 'Just to hear you mention *Divali* makes me think of *jalebis*.'

'Can you make them?'

'Yes, I learned, but I haven't made any for years. This will give me an excuse to try.'

'Plan on staying a while. People are thinking of playing cards after dinner.'

To celebrate Saturday properly as *Divali* Guddo spent the whole day cleaning to welcome Lakshmi. She took great care in making lots of *jalebis*, and even though their shape was a little irregular they tasted fine. Before setting out for Gita's she performed the ritual worship at home. She had always kept a picture of Lakshmi with her. But inside the apartment there was no place to light the lamps, no special area set aside for the ritual, no *tulsi*, no altar, nor even any windows. She placed the candles and the lamps shaped from dough right in the worship tray, and another candle in the sink close to the tap.

When Guddo and Raju started out for Gita's place, everything outside seemed terribly deserted. As always, the neon streetlamps were there, but no lamps or shops bright with sweets, no exploding firecrackers or brilliant fireworks. This *Divali*, this festival of lamps without any lamps, depressed Guddo a great deal.

Not that they didn't have their own kind of *Divali* here. Every Fourth of July the city resounded with explosions like a war zone. When at twilight the fireworks lit up the sky with colourful bouquets and showered down golden sparks, the whole city seemed to be making merry. People streamed out of their houses to gather near this festival of lights. Guddo too had gone to Battery Park to see the fireworks set off out in the harbour near the Statue of Liberty. But she hadn't been able to feel any sort of inner gladness, she had no sense deep within herself of experiencing the celebration. It was nothing more than a spectacle.

Gita's apartment was bright and festive. Gita herself was resplendent in a blue Banarsi sari edged with gold brocade; she had made up her face with great care and wore turquoise-studded gold earrings to match her sari. Guddo marvelled at how beautiful she looked; even now her figure was as slim and trim as before her marriage, and with her make-up she had concealed the faint circles below her eyes and the first fine wrinkles that had begun to appear.

Radhika and Kanika were radiant too in silk *kurta-pajama*. Although this was Kanika's last year of school and Radhika was in the ninth grade, both looked almost grown-up.

When Guddo's eyes suddenly met Pinki's she quickly turned her face away. Her ears began to burn, she felt a strange commotion in her stomach. Since she had moved from Pinki's apartment they had not even spoken on the telephone. If either one had to send anything to the other, they did it through Gita. Gita, busy with her duties as hostess, had not yet realised that her two sisters were avoiding one another, but when she became aware of the tension on both their faces, she told each one separately to go to her bedroom. Gathering Pinki and Guddo together in her arms, she said, 'On *Divali* all quarrels must have an end.'

The sisters embraced amid tears and laughter. How much affection was still left in both of them! After living in the same city for years they hadn't exchanged a single word until now. To

Guddo it seemed as though a great weight had been lifted from her heart, and she felt suddenly healed and light. They talked and talked, catching up on the last two and a half years.

The other guests were gathering in the living room. Now Gita felt she must separate her sisters. 'So many other people have come,' she said, 'be sure to talk to them too. Come along, we'll go in the other room. We have to perform the ritual soon or dinner will be much too late.'

At one end of the living room a sheet had been spread, on it were set pictures and images of Lakshmi and Ganesh, Ram, Lakshman and Sita. On a large tray garlands, corn, sugarcane, fruit, coconuts and sweets were set before the images. In a small silver tray Gita had put a little lamp moulded from dough, holy water, saffron and silver rupees, a gift from their mother. Biji had given each of the three sisters ten silver coins from the time of the Raj for worshipping Lakshmi on *Divali*. That day Biji herself would write the Ganesh and Gayatri *mantras* on the walls and wash the image of Lakshmi with ambrosia of milk and saffron: these silver coins were Lakshmi made visible. All night they had lain in the worship tray; next morning they would be wiped, tied together in a little bundle and hidden away among the clothes stacked in a large black trunk, which was always kept securely locked. For Guddo her mother's trunk had always represented a mystery or a treasure. Whenever she saw her opening it, Guddo would come and squat by it, and her curious eyes would spy all kinds of little bundles strewn here and there among the masses of folded silk saris and suits. But Biji forbade her ever to touch anything. Then she herself would open up some little package and show it to Guddo.

'These are real pearls. Your father brought them from Madras. I'll have a necklace made of them and give it to you on your wedding day.'

But afterwards all the packages were untied, for Biji too enjoyed opening up and rewrapping all the wonders in her treasure chest. She had stored away so many things for her daughters' dowries – rugs, cotton sheets, embroidered tableclothes, bedspreads, shawls, silver trays, gold jewelry – which she had picked up whenever she had time for shopping.

Guddo had often heard her father say, 'You're putting all these things away to give to the girls, but by the time they've grown up all the fashions will be completely different.'

'Just let me keep on with it,' Biji would answer, 'we have three daughters to marry. When the time comes where could we get all the money we'll need in a hurry?'

'But my dear, why are you worrying about it? Your three girls are beautiful. When they're grown up, prospective bridgegrooms will be fighting for the chance to take them away.'

When Gita began to recite the Gayatri verse all the others joined in to chant it with her. Pinki and Guddo sat beside her to perform the ritual. Happy, Guddo was saying to herself that the only real holiday pleasure she experienced was in these Indian religious festivals.

After dinner the card games started and went on until early Sunday morning. No one was worried about having to get up early. Gathered together in an alien country on this Festival of Lamps without lamps, they celebrated by lighting up their sweet memories of the past.

Gita introduced a young man to Guddo and said, 'Arun's a good friend of ours. I've asked him to drop you off at your apartment on his way home.'

When Guddo and Raju were outside Gita's apartment building Arun led them up to a parked yellow taxi and asked them to get in. Guddo was astonished, and Raju burst out, 'But uncle, this is a taxi!'

'It is,' said Arun, laughing, 'but there'll be no tax for you.'

'You mean it's yours?'

'One hundred per cent mine. Why, don't you think I look as though I own it?'

In fact, Arun appeared to be such a polite and cultured young fellow that it was difficult for Guddo to understand how he could be a taxi-driver. 'But what do you actually do?' she asked.

'What do you mean, actually? You're looking at it! I drive a taxi.'

'I meant . . .'

'Maybe you've just come from India? That's why you're so flustered talking to me. But I'm used to that.'

Guddo was afraid she'd hurt his feelings.

'I'm not flustered,' she said. 'Just surprised, that's all. Because you just don't look like . . .'

'But it's *Divali*, right? So I wore my best clothes. But you were right anyway – the fact is, when I finished my engineering degree I came here for three months on a tourist visa. Then I thought, why not look for work here, especially since in India I wasn't able to find a decent job. Only here, wherever I applied they refused to give me anything without a work permit. So with a recommendation from the relatives I'm staying with I got a job as a waiter in an Indian restaurant. I got paid twenty-five dollars a day, plus tips, and had my meals free. There were a couple of other Indian waiters so I felt at home – illegals like me. One day the immigration officials raided the restaurant and we were all arrested and put in jail.'

Raju and Guddo both found these revelations disturbing.

Arun smiled and said to Raju, 'But this isn't anything to tell you about. How old are you?'

'I'm just twelve.'

'Do you have a girlfriend?'

Raju, who had no real friends at all, was mortified.

'Well, it doesn't matter,' Arun said, and went on with his story. He'd met a girl named Judy. A friend advised him that if he married an American girl he would get his green card. At the time he hadn't even considered such a move, but when his appeal came up before the judge he said that he had a fiancée and was staying on in America to marry her. When Judy was called to witness, she confirmed his story. Understandably, Arun felt profoundly grateful to her.

They decided to marry right away. Everything was done in such haste that he had not even had time to tell his parents about it. They had been insisting that he come back to India to marry, for they had already looked over several girls for him. So Arun took time to go back to India to see his mother and father. He told his parents he didn't find the girls to his liking, but he didn't tell them he already had a wife in America. When they asked him if this was the case he denied it. He felt constantly pulled in two directions. He was an only son, so he felt he couldn't shatter their dreams, but he couldn't hurt Judy either.

'Uncle,' Raju asked, 'when did you get the taxi?'

'Well, after Judy and I were married she applied for a loan. I still didn't have a job. I thought, why not open a transportation company? Raju, my friend, I'm not a taxi-driver but the owner of the A and J Transportation Company. And that's what I've told everybody in India too, so families of marriageable girls keep coming to inquire. Actually, it's neither the whole truth nor a lie. I don't hire the taxi I drive, I own it outright. When I've got a little money together I'll buy some more taxis and hire drivers, so then I'll be the owner of a company, right? But to tell the truth, this isn't really the profession I prefer. It gets very boring sitting behind the steering wheel all day. I probably won't be able to stand this kind of work for very long.'

Listening to Arun, Guddo was uneasy. How quickly he had got on to intimate terms with them! But she found him attractive, and she was pleased that he and Raju seemed to be communicating so well too.

Guddo's apartment was not very far away, but while he talked Arun drove very slowly.

'What does Judy do?' she asked him.

'She's a secretary in a small firm.'

'May I ask a personal question? How does it feel to be married to a foreigner?'

'That's very hard to answer. Sometimes you feel very out of place right in your own apartment. Everything there is according to Judy's taste. I'm an object according to Judy's taste too. My place in that house is definitely secondary. I don't feel like the master of the household, the way a man should in his own home. It's as though the house is Judy's, and I'm just putting up there like a guest. I've thought about getting a divorce because I'm still thinking I might marry an Indian girl and start a family the right way. That's why I haven't asked my parents to stop looking for a girl.'

Once again Guddo thought it all very disturbing – even frightening.

Eleven

It had begun to snow. Guddo fondly remembered Chandigarh and its warm winter afternoons. She used to like to set a *charpoy* out on the lawn and bask in the sunshine; then, when she heard the voice of a hawker, call him over and buy roasted peanuts, puffed rice, or sesame brittle to munch on; or she would buy oranges from the fruit peddler, salt them and drink the juice from each slice, or sometimes, peeling sugarcane with her teeth, suck out the juice, or else stop the juice vendor and drink the cane juice with lime and rock salt – these were the little things so sweet to experience again when they came into focus in the camera of her memory. Sometimes a neighbour would come to sit with her or perhaps, calling from another lawn, ask how she was, or at times a distant relation would visit. Guests every day, with no waiting! But here it was impossible for anyone to visit without giving advance notice, formally telephoning to arrange the time for meeting. She could not even call on her sisters without an 'appointment', so Guddo suffered here from the lack of ease and informality even among the members of her own family.

In only a week the new year would begin. The whole city was brightly decorated and everyone was enjoying the pleasures of the Christmas season. This was when New York celebrated its real *Divali*, and continuously too for several days. The branches of the trees were covered with thousands of tiny, colourful electric bulbs, and how lovely the lines of trees along the streets appeared, festooned for miles with clusters of twinkling stars. And in the shop windows, the huge flower-like red leaves of the

poinsettias and the gift boxes wrapped in shiny green and red –
Guddo found all this very beautiful. A white blanket of snow
covered the park; here and there the green of pine needles peeked
through and made the whiteness even more dazzling. The whole
atmosphere was painted in just these three colours – the bleak-
ness of the winter season brightened with green and red, with a
background to make them stand out provided by the canvas of
white snow.

As soon as the weather cleared a little, vendors of warm socks,
woollen hats, mufflers and gloves spread their wares out on the
sidewalk for sale. It was crowded everywhere, there was hardly
room to walk in the shops or streets. Advertisements for the latest
Christmas gift plans were hung outside the shops and constantly
roared over radio and television. In this cold weather vendors of
hot dogs, hot pretzels and roasted chestnuts stood on the
sidewalks all day long. It seemed that in the smoky, murky and
colourless atmosphere of winter everybody in the city was
working together to make it bright – for otherwise how could
they get through this long cold spell? Everywhere you looked
people kept busy devising one artificial scheme after another to
render life better, more pleasurable, the whole of society wasting
its entire existence in finding new methods for being happy.
Newer and newer machines were invented to make every job
easier, and then one became a machine for earning money to buy
one of those machines.

Guddo too was trapped in this same machine. She was so
involved in finishing her studies as quickly as possible, earning a
decent income and settling her children here, that she had no
time at all to think of herself.

Juneja was on the phone. 'What are you doing for New Year's
Eve?' he asked her.

'Haven't even thought about it. Nothing, most likely.'

'In that case come and spend the evening with us. Don't plan
anything else. I'll come straight from the office and pick you up.'

*

52

Outside it was getting colder. The weather had turned stormy and a sharp wind was blowing up the snow in swirls. Guddo's basement was like a fridge. Hands and feet stayed chilled even under the quilt. For some reason, maybe because of the snowfall, the central heating had broken down. To help them through it the landlord had brought an electric heater. Nothing for it but to sit huddled close to the heater, with teeth chattering, and not leave it for a minute.

Once more the phone rang.

'Plans have changed a bit. Ramna has had to go to India. And my mother's gone to my brother's in Michigan. So our party here at home has been cancelled. I'm sorry.'

'But I understand, it's quite all right.'

'But if you don't mind, we two could go out somewhere to celebrate.'

Guddo found herself in a predicament. 'But if you're cancelling . . .'

'No, it's boring to just sit around at home. If you're bored on New Year's Eve then the whole year will turn out badly. So one really has to do something. Get ready and we'll go out somewhere for dinner. Okay?'

For New Year's Eve Guddo wore a blue Conjeeveram sari with a contrasting pink border; this was her favourite. She put on only light make-up, with a blue *bindi* on her forehead. For her lipstick she chose a pink to match her sari border; she used very little perfume and wound her long hair neatly in a bun. As soon as Juneja saw her he said, 'You're looking very beautiful tonight.'

Guddo broke into a smile, her eyes lit up, and the heavy burden of her years seemed to fall away.

In Juneja's behaviour that evening Guddo was aware of a new kind of openness and informality.

'Tell me, what kind of restaurant would you like?' he asked her. 'French, Italian, Chinese or Indian?'

'Dr Juneja, I really don't know anything about restaurants here. Wherever you like . . .'

'Well, first of all, you must stop calling me "Dr Juneja". My name is Chandar. People at the hospital just call me "Chet", but I hope you'll pronounce it correctly.'

'I think I'll call you "Chet" too!'

'If you like – but tomorrow don't say that this fellow is a half-breed.'

Suddenly Guddo felt her forehead throbbing. Why had Juneja used that word 'half-breed'? In this man's mind too there must be some kind of problem with the ego. How many Indians had accepted a foreign version of their names to make them easier for others to pronounce! But in their hearts there remained a sense of uneasiness and loss. Guddo wanted to keep these moments light and enjoyable, she didn't want to make too much of this matter. She said, 'Then please call me Uma. How would that be in place of "Mrs Chaddha"?'

'Certainly. And there's nothing "half-breed" in that!'

Guddo hesitated for just a moment. Juneja was in high spirits tonight, and she too found herself talking very freely. The walls were falling down, the streams were ready to overflow. Nothing could hold her back tonight. Only the walls of the mind . . . these were still very strong.

She had no idea who made the decision or when but a little while later she found herself in a French restaurant, seated facing Juneja. French cuisine was only a name to her and she could make nothing of the menu, where everything was written in French. After she had puzzled over it for a while Juneja leaned toward her and said:

'The hors-d'oeuvres, with asparagus soup for the first course, and poached salmon for the entrée are very good here. Won't you try them?'

Guddo was relieved. 'Whatever you choose will be fine for me.'

'Then I'll also order whatever wine you like.'

'But I don't drink.'

'No matter, just tell me if you prefer red or white.'

'In my religion it's a sin to drink.'

'What's your religion?'

54

'I didn't meant that, really. I only meant . . . in any religion stealing, drinking liquor, they're all considered evil.'

'But wine isn't really liquor. According to the Bible it's the purest drink in the world.'

'Oh, you don't have to quote scripture or the Puranas! I suppose I can have something to drink too, it's not officially forbidden.'

Guddo had no idea what she was eating. All these novel sensations from the combination of food, wine and Juneja were making her dizzy, and still she was eager to assimilate every new experience.

When they left the restaurant Juneja looked at his watch and said, 'It's only nine o'clock. Shall we go to a bar?'

'I can't drink anything more!'

'Then tell me what you'd like to do.'

Guddo was silent. Then Juneja said, 'Come on, let's go home. We can be comfortable there while we talk.'

Guddo's feet weren't touching the ground. She seemed to be flying. She felt like a wisp of cotton floating in the breeze, a drifting bubble. For a moment she lost her footing. Juneja quickly reached out to catch her. She felt his arms around her shoulders, steadying her as she walked. When they were sitting in the car Juneja took her hand and pressed it between his own. He said, 'How are you feeling?'

Guddo smiled. She felt a tender warmth spreading through her, and with it a sense of helplessness. Juneja had an apartment in Manhattan, where he stayed over when he had a lot of work at the hospital. After she came upstairs in the elevator, with Juneja's arms around her, and entered the apartment she fell back on a sofa.

Delightfully intoxicated, in the dim bluish lamplight, she felt she was Juneja's prisoner. Her body trembled as he passed his hand very gently over it, as though tracing out a flower. Languorous, half-unconscious, Guddo was aware only of every movement of that hand on her body, every touch of those fingers, each pressure of that other body. She was in another world. Within her closed eyes every perception, every scent and taste

55

floated like a dreamy scene where so many images blurred into another. The living touch of her husband, the unsatisfied imagined union with her dead husband's corpse, Batra's incomplete shadow. Then the picture would disappear, leaving only a vague impression behind. A sense of the present. The awareness of a desired man's powerful and tender possession.

Everything around Guddo seemed completely new, ever changing and overwhelming. As though she had reached her destination after years of wandering. In her barren life tender leaves had begun to sprout.

That night Guddo was alone in the basement apartment as Raju had gone to celebrate New Year's Eve with Gita's children and stay overnight there. All night long Guddo's body trembled. Things of the past shrivelled and expanded in the present. A sense of regret began to colour the experience of pleasure and triumph. The sense of losing and finding mingled together. Her heart would leap up and then someone, something, would pounce on it. Where am I going? she wondered. What's my destination? The road wasn't easy, and maybe not even the right one either.

In a life spent mostly without a man Guddo had developed a strange sort of strength, which made it possible for her to fight and keep her head above water. Whenever there had been a man he was on the sidelines, never at the centre. Now suddenly she had begun to be aware of weakness. She felt it would be good for someone else to manage things, good to cast all the burdens of her body and heart on someone else. But she had to think also what a mistake this could be. Was a relationship of any kind at all possible with a married man like Juneja? Could these few moments of pleasure in being close to him provide a basis for any stable relationship? And would Juneja too be thinking as seriously about her as she was about him? She spent hours battling with these questions. Come back, Guddo, come back to yourself! The truth of life is a cold basement room, an unending barren round of work, worries, and problems, and don't forget it!

Twelve

In the last week of Guddo's accounting course the instructor set up a couple of job interviews for her. During this time classes in personality and presentation were also offered, along with counselling on how to correct one's personal defects. Guddo's instructor advised her to have her hair cut short; and she said it would be more professional if she wore a business suit to her interviews. She was industrious, the instructor said, she was intelligent, but one had to have a good personality too to get a good job. At first Guddo was upset. She had to arrange marriages for two daughters – what would people say? But the teacher was just speaking from her own experience. After a lot of hesitation Guddo made an appointment with a hairdresser. When her hair was cut shoulder-length and set, Guddo herself agreed that she looked fine. After all her classmates congratulated her, her self-confidence grew.

But in her search for a position Guddo suffered many setbacks. She was turned away by every office where she hoped for a job with a mid-range salary. At some places she was aware that possibly her Indian accent in English was the problem because the interviewers asked her several times to repeat what she'd said. But when she clipped her speech in the American way and pronounced her 'a's' flat in words like 'can't' or said 'ain't', she sounded peculiar, even ridiculous. In her heart she was pained by this schizophrenic speech. Why should she go on imitating anybody else? But her own natural way of speaking was not effective. She had studied for the most part not in English-medium but in Arya Samaj schools; still, she had an MA in

English. Her knowledge of the language and her command of vocabulary were better than many Americans', but because she was not accustomed to speaking it she lacked fluency. Her syntax was influenced by Hindi, and her vocabulary and pronunciation were closer to British English. Following her instructor's suggestion, Guddo began to stand in front of a mirror to practise American speech. She would make up a dialogue, using American gestures, with shoulders raised high. But in very little time this got on her nerves; she let her shoulders drop and said – using an American idiom she'd learned from her fellow students – 'To hell with it!' In the past she had made fun of Pinki's American accent; now she was obliged to talk the same way. Raju thought her practising was highly amusing. He was still in the process of formation and he had learned his English in school. It had not taken him long to pick up the differences in pronunciation, so he would tease her saying, 'Mummy, you don't say *shedule*, you have to say *skedule*.'

After a lot of running around Guddo found a job in a bank as an ordinary accounting clerk. Her fellow student, a black girl named Georgina, though she needed a job even more than Guddo, still had not found work. At twenty-two, Georgina had four children, whose father neither lived with them nor acknowledged any responsibility towards the children; and as the two of them had never married, Georgina could make no legal claims on his support. Guddo sympathised with her having to miss class every other day to look after a sick child or take it to the hospital. Georgina came to depend on Guddo, who was at the head of the class, for her notes and support.

One evening, after Guddo had been studying late in the reading room, when she left to go home, outside the school she found Georgina screaming insults at somebody. Guddo had witnessed fights like this in India, but never here before. Insults even more violent than the ones in Panjabi. Perhaps Georgina too was somebody's illegitimate child. The next day Georgina herself told Guddo that her boyfriend wouldn't give her a cent. On the contrary, now that he was out of work, he came to beg some money from her. With her scholarship she wasn't able even to feed the children properly, so how was she going to give him anything? He'd spend it all on liquor anyway.

In Guddo's class the students were black, Asian or Hispanic, not one of them was white. They ranged in age from twenty to fifty. From their appearance it wasn't easy to guess anybody's age. As for Guddo, people regularly underestimated her age; especially when she was wearing a sari no one could guess it. But when, on one occasion, she dressed up in a fine sari to go for an appointment at an employment agency, a secretary there got talking with her and said, 'You really look terrific in that outfit, dear, but it just won't do if you want to get a job in an American office.'

In slacks or skirt Guddo thought she looked like somebody else. Hybrid speech, now hybrid style of dress. She felt that American clothes didn't suit her body. She was built so that in sari or *kurta* her figure looked fine but in American clothes her stomach seemed to stick out. It happened that here the Chinese, Japanese, Vietnamese or people from any other country all dressed in American clothes, whatever kind of figure they might have. But South Asian women were more cautious in such matters and wanted to wear only the sari or *kurta-pajama*. On the other hand, slacks or skirt sometimes served in a protective capacity for Guddo. Especially while she was working as a salesgirl, when she didn't want to be recognised by some Indian, the sari would have made that difficult. If some curious Indian questioned her she would answer vaguely, saying sometimes she was from Pakistan, at others from Africa, but never said who she really was. Guddo's identity, her sense of self, was assured only by her sari, and it became natural for her to change clothes as soon as she returned home from the office.

Pinki was happy that at the library there was no particular concern about how one dressed, but all the same, to avoid being very conspicuous, she did not wear a sari, and anyway, it didn't seem professional. As for the growing children, dressing in Indian clothes was becoming a problem. Radhika constantly fought with

Gita about it. Once, for a school function, Gita forced her to wear *kurta-pajama* sent over by her brother-in-law. When she came home Radhika said, speaking English as usual, 'Mummy, I felt very uncomfortable in this outfit, but . . .'

'But *kya?*' Gita answered, mixing up the two languages.

'I did get some compliments from people.'

'Darling, didn't I tell you? Don't underestimate the value of the things that are really yours. The more you try to know Indian culture the more you'll realise how glorious it is. What do they have in this country? Their whole history is only two hundred years old. You ought to feel proud of being Indian.'

'You've started lecturing, Mom!'

'You're calling me "Mom" again. Why can't you just call me "Mummy"?'

'"Mummy" sounds like Egyptian mummies – dead bodies.'

'I don't know anything about all that. We simply go by the meaning it has in India.'

'But "Mummy" isn't Indian, it's British. It's "Biji" in India, isn't it?'

Guddo had to laugh at Radhika's answer; at the same time she thought how ignorant these children who had grown up here were becoming about their Indian language and traditions.

Being Indian was turning into Radhika's biggest problem. At home and with her relatives everything went smoothly, but when she was with her school friends she felt ashamed of her Indianness. She would take ham and cheese or salami sandwiches to school but never parathas, even if she had to go hungry.

Kanika was not at all like that. She never tried to hide the fact that she was Indian. She was very intelligent, quick in understanding, and ahead of everybody in her class. Her classmates often expressed their admiration for her; but she did not have a lot of girlfriends. Kanika possessed a natural confidence about her own identity. It may have been a characteristic inherited from her father that she asserted herself as an Indian – even though this was a claim not so much of being an Indian as of being Kanika. She had always had a feeling of being somehow special, a feeling nourished both at home and outside.

Ashok was considered special because he was a boy. As for Radhika, she was intelligent too but in comparison with her sister she appeared very mediocre to the rest of the family. Because she had never been able to find her own place at home she had from the very beginning sought a place away from it. Whenever any friend or relative visited, the talk was mostly of Kanika, of how bright she was and what a certain professor had said, the prize she'd received, the subject she was studying, how she'd decided to become a doctor, and the like.

Radhika's world was made up of her numerous girlfriends. She would spend time at their houses, or they would all congregate on the sidewalk in front of her apartment or in the park. These girls from her class came from many backgrounds – Jewish, Hispanic, or fourth generation 'WASP' families. Out of the eleven nine had parents who were divorced. Since for the most part both the parents of each of the girls lived in New York, the children divided their time between them, spending the school week with the mothers and the weekends with the fathers. These daughters of broken homes were of a strangely carefree, rude and boorish type. It was their nature to scream when they spoke, use common profanity in their conversation, and answer any question with insolence. It happened that the father of one of these girls had just married for the third time. When Gita asked her how she felt about it she answered, 'I don't give a damn.' The unspoken hurt was clear in her answer. She had adopted this same hostile attitude toward the whole of society.

Gita had begun to fear that Radhika too would become like these girls, insolent, sloppy and hostile. But it was not possible to separate Radhika from her companions. They were her whole life. Immediately after school she would fall in with their plans to go somewhere together. If she was at home, she would be talking to them on the telephone. If you tried to stop her she would answer, 'I'm talking about my homework – if you don't want me to do it just say so.'

Answers like this began to get on Gita's nerves. When she sometimes tried to explain to her that she should be polite and modest like Kanika, Radhika would be even more provoked. 'I can't stand all this tyranny and it's all because of Kanika. You're always praising her, you take her side no matter how much at fault she is, no matter how unjust it is to me. Why do you want me to be a loner like her?'

Radhika started addressing her sister with terms like 'terror' and 'bore'.

Guddo was still living at Gita's when Jijaji once slapped Radhika violently. Guddo had never before seen big girls struck that way by their fathers. Her own father had never so much as lifted his hand against any girl. To be sure, her brothers sometimes got a beating, but striking or fighting with the daughters was solely the mother's job.

The problem that came up next was both trivial and important – it was all in the point of view. There was to be a 'slumber party' at the house of one of Radhika's friends. Gita had given her permission for Radhika to spend the night there but when Jijaji heard about it he said, 'If you let her spend the night out like this how can you tell if she'll be with other girls or with boys? Don't let her get accustomed to slumber parties like this.'

In protest Radhika yelled, 'I told them days ago that I was going to come. What are they going to think? I can't ditch them!'

For Radhika the most important thing was her companions. How could she make them angry? That was her society, and for Radhika their friendship was proof of her social acceptance. The least little thing they said provided the horizons of her existence. She felt that her parents understood nothing about life here. They were always giving orders. 'Talk this way, be like that, dress that way, don't go there!' They wanted to burden her with all their Indian customs and traditions. But she couldn't follow their ways and end up like Kanika without a single friend.

Jijaji was saying, 'So you can't make your friends angry because they're more important than us! What we say doesn't matter at all.'

Radhika stamped her foot. 'I don't care! I'm going.'

At this Jijaji really lost his temper and started slapping her over and over again while he shouted, 'Shameless thing, talking back to me! I'm going to knock all that insolence out of you. I never even raised an eyebrow at my father – and you dare to talk like that, "I don't care!" If those words ever come out of your mouth again I won't stop till I've broken every bone in your body! This is what you're learning in school. Your mother and father can just go on jabbering and you'll do whatever you please. I'm telling you, I'm your father and you're going to have to pay attention to everything I say. There'll be no talking back. You're not providing for me yet but if you go on like this who knows how you'll look after us when I'm really old?'

Radhika never got to go to the slumber party. She kept the fierce power of her rage boiling inside her. If she let it explode it would only invite more beatings. But to herself she said over and over again, 'I hate him, I hate him!'

As much as possible she kept away from her father. Even earlier there had been little communication between the two of them. His working hours were so irregular that he would be leaving the house when the children came home. Weekends were when he usually met with the children, or, when it was necessary, he would call them from work, particularly to talk with Gita or Kanika.

Jijaji had a lot of respect for Kanika. He was so impressed with her intelligence that he considered her decisions more important than his own. He felt that by coming to this country at such an advanced age he had wasted time and opportunities and that he no longer had the capacity to understand the way of doing things here so that he could accomplish something worthwhile. Working as a doorman was only a makeshift arrangement, but gradually he began to feel that he could find no better job than this. He no longer had the energy to do all the running around required if he was to start a business. In a way, by regarding himself as inferior and a failure he had achieved a compromise with himself. Now Kanika had become the centre for his repressed ambitions and aspirations.

He encouraged her to study medicine. Every immigrant felt that in this country the vocation of medicine made a person extremely rich. Therefore they all, whether Korean, Japanese or Indian, pushed their children in this direction to try to improve

63

their livelihood. For Jijaji too his greatest profit-earning investment for the future was Kanika's education, so he devoted all his
attention to her since the other two children had not given any
proof of being as brilliant. Still, he kept telling them to be like
her and offered her as a role model every time she won a prize.

For Kanika this was beginning to turn into a burden. In order
to keep up to the level of her parents' aspirations she had to
suppress many of the natural wishes of her young age and work
relentlessly to achieve first place continually in every subject.
Worry over her studies preyed on her mind constantly and her
health began to deteriorate. Gita began to scold her about her
poor appetite.

'If you don't eat how can you study? You lose your appetite
whenever it's time to eat. I won't take no for an answer today.
I've made all the things you like. Your favourite vegetables and
spicy curry. If you don't eat, your father will be very upset, you
do realise that, don't you?'

The more Gita insisted, the more miserable Kanika felt. But
as the family regarded her as more and more important, she
began to consider herself entitled to even more respect. Neither
her parents nor her brother and sister seemed to her able to
claim equality with her. No matter what was going on at home,
it seemed that she was in charge of everything. She began to
have the same attitude toward everyone who came to visit as
well.

Guddo thought Kanika conceited. When you talked with her
she was gentle and courteous, but it was clear from her attitude
that she considered everybody else beneath her. Because of her
command of English she used words in such a way that on the
surface their sting was not apparent but they struck home all the
same. While she was looking for a job Guddo had often heard
talk like this, where it was possible to say harsh things sweetly
just with a few expressions, like what that secretary at the
employment agency had said.

At home only Radhika stood up to Kanika and refused to let
her dominate her. She wanted to live like a free and unrestrained

64

American girl and have nothing at all to do with Indian tradition and customs.

Why were her parents so tradition-bound? she wondered. Why wouldn't they let her do what she wanted? The parents of the other girls gave them all the freedom they wanted, so why did hers restrict her like this without any reason?

Radhika was beginning to shape a new world of her own. Her name would be Sally . . . No, maybe Janie or Laura would be nicer. Her mother and father were Mr and Mrs Johnson.

One day she said to them, 'Can I change my name to Laura in school?'

'Where did you pick up such nonsense!'

'What's so bad about changing your name?'

Suddenly Jijaji slapped her hard. 'Don't you understand anything?' he said. 'If you change your name then tell me, how are you related to us? If that's what you want, then change your name and after that, change your skin – but how can you change your soul?'

'But my soul's already changed, long before,' Radhika said sarcastically. Jijaji was alarmed – maybe after all there was some truth in what she was saying.

She had already begun to ask her friends to call her Laura. And Gita, when she met one of Radhika's friends while they were shopping in some store, found herself introduced as 'Mrs Johnson'. About to correct the mistake, she was interrupted by Radhika, who started to explain to her in broken Hindi: 'Mummy, as a joke I told them my name was Laura Johnson. What else can I do, nobody can understand these Indian names. Everybody used to call me "Rattika". Isn't that hilarious?'

Gita laughed when she heard Radhika mispronouncing her own name like that, but she also was aware of some foreboding. Guddo, for her part, thought it was a good thing in a way for Radhika to be assimilating into life here. It would be easier for her to adjust in the future, while Raju, by comparison, remained utterly alone, cut off from most human contacts. His closest friends were Gita's children, and on weekends or holidays he would go to visit Ashok and play football with him. As for his classmates, his association with them was limited to time spent at school. Guddo realised that he was reluctant to invite his friends home simply because of the basement. Raju denied this, but perhaps only because he wanted to avoid hurting his mother. Therefore Guddo's first task as soon as she had found a job was to start looking for a better apartment. Furthermore, Anima, her eldest daughter, would be completing her exams in a couple of months and she would have to send her a ticket to come to America.

After she'd been working a few months Guddo rented a four-room apartment for three hundred dollars a month. The landlord also sold her all the furniture, which was quite decent, for another five hundred. If you looked closely you might see that it was a bit dirty, a bit shabby, with a few stains here and there, but from a distance it looked perfectly fine. The window curtains and the wall-to-wall carpeting appeared freshly washed.

Guddo would be moving into her new home on the first of July. The idea thrilled her. Now she would be able to invite anybody she wanted. Even Dr Juneja. True, it wasn't any match for his palace, but it would at least look like a habitation of human beings, whereas while they lived at the other place it had begun to feel as though they had exchanged their human form for some other kind of creature. Now both Guddo and Raju would each have their own room. The third room was made into the living room, while the dining table was set in the kitchen. The rooms were small but big enough for them both. When Anima came they would manage – she would share a room with either Raju or Guddo.

66

Thirteen

The first thing Guddo did after she moved was to invite Gita and
Pinki and their families to dinner. Only Radhika did not come
because, Gita said, she'd made plans with her girlfriends. Gita
felt there was nothing she could do about it, though, as Guddo
understood, she nevertheless tried very hard to bring Radhika.
Not that it was any great matter if the girl didn't come, but
Guddo suddenly realised that she herself would not have to put
up with such teenage problems where her own daughters were
concerned.

It seemed as though Anima and Tanima had reached college
age in the twinkling of an eye. Guddo, of course, preoccupied
with her own daily routine, might simply not have noticed. But
from the time following her husband's death she had always been
very close to the children, and her daughters shared everything
with her, no matter how trifling. Guddo had shaped them both
according to her own strict morality. Anima, the eldest, was
strongly influenced by her mother, relying deeply on her standard
of conduct and her self-sacrificing nature. Without a father, her
mother was everything to Anima; both at home and away she
had full confidence in her direction and example. Guddo had so
thoroughly instilled her opinions and manners in her that they
had become her own as well.

Anima had also begun to share in the family problems, taking
on responsibility for her sister after Guddo left for America.
Although there was only a two years' difference between the two
girls, Anima would interrogate Tanima just like her mother:
'You're sure you don't need any money?' Or, 'Don't you miss

Mummy? Next Sunday I'll take you to a movie.' And she described all that was going on in long letters to Guddo.

'Mummy, you mustn't worry. I'm very happy with my friends here at the hostel. Tanima is still first in class at the medical college. By the way, she has a friend there. It may be serious. She'll write you about it herself.'

That word 'friend' startled Guddo. Different emotions sprang up in her mind all at once: a nameless fear for her daughters, a near-forgotten memory of her own youth . . . God help us! If only everything turned out all right. Praying in her heart, Guddo looked at Raju. How happy she would be when she had her daughters with her in her own house. She'd forgotten how badly the two girls got along and how much they quarrelled.

No matter, for the moment her memories were all sweetness. In her daughters' letters there was no mention of any squabbling. It seemed as though the two of them had suddenly grown up.

Before Guddo's eyes spread the dawn light of her reunited family. How much her own it seemed, how familiar, that Indian dawn, decorated with birds in golden sunlight. Birdsong provided her morning alarm clock, the milkman's cry finished waking her. After that the whole succession of morning sounds began – the rustle of brooms on the street, the crackle of swept-up leaves, the tinkling bells of bicycles and rickshaws, the solemn call of vendors – 'Bibiji, please buy my vegetables,' 'Bibiji, fresh bread for sale!' Suddenly all Guddo's senses were excited by the memory of these familiar sounds.

And how empty the mornings here seemed to her now. Inside the apartment with its drawn curtains one was not even aware when it was morning. After you were wakened by some rock music or advertisement shouted out on the radio you had to rush to get ready to go to work: put the kettle on to boil while you brushed your teeth, and all the rest of it. Outside on the street swiftly passing cars, the terrible racket of the trucks, the nerve-shattering thunder of the elevated trains crossing the bridge, as though every morning meant violence and violation.

In winter even the morning light was greyish, the sky cloudy, or hazy with dirty snow. Neither the scent of grass washed with fresh dew, nor the wet fragrance of flowers and green leaves. Everything made of cement. Brick and concrete buildings, concrete streets, concrete houses. If you walked by a Jewish delicatessen near the grocery store there was a sudden smell of coffee, blending in the air the greasy odour of eggs frying for breakfast at the fast-food eateries, sausage, potatoes fried with onions, buttered toast. Heaped together here and there on the sidewalks huge black plastic bags filled with garbage that stank as they waited for the Department of Sanitation trucks to pick them up. Every morning when she confronted these piled-up garbage bags Guddo remembered the filthy open sewers of Indian cities and said to herself, 'Back home we don't make such violent efforts to stay clean.'

On these same sidewalks she had also seen frightening images of the homeless, half-crazed, only half-human, wrapped in stinking rags. It shocked her that on the steps of the buildings in this country so devoted to wealth and humanity there could live such disgraceful examples of unfortunate mankind.

One evening when Guddo returned home from Manhattan with Raju, late because of shopping, the cold wind was gusting so strong that even in her overcoat she felt the chill. On the way she saw somebody in rags trying to make a bed on the sidewalk in front of a shop by spreading out some old, torn blankets.

Raju said, 'He'll die in this cold. Let's take him home.'

Guddo felt sickened by the stench that came from the man. But she didn't want to discourage Raju's generous impulse. She said, 'All right, let's take him with us – but I'm sure he won't agree.'

'Let's find out! I'll ask him.' Raju spoke to him then in English. 'Do you have any place to stay near here? Will you come home with us?'

The man didn't even look up. Perhaps it sounded to him like the usual noises of people passing in the street. As he got no answer Raju was about to repeat his question when a passer-by said to him, 'Don't try to talk to him. He's drunk and probably crazy.' And Guddo took hold of Raju's shoulders and pulled him away.

69

'If he's really crazy or drunk he might hit you, so just leave him alone. There's no point in getting involved. You know what they say – "Help somebody and get kicked for it." Come along now, let's not have any trouble.'

Tugging at Raju's coat, Guddo was moving toward the subway entrance, but Raju hadn't finished with his attempt at philanthropy.

'If everyone's afraid to help these people because they may be drunk or crazy, then won't they die?'

'Look, Raju! You don't have to be charitable at the risk of your life. Anyway, we're not so much better off ourselves, we're just about getting by. We're not expected to do anything for these people. Why don't the millionaires in this country help out? When we have heaps of money then we'll do something.'

'My sociology teacher says that there's some risk in everything we do, even in helping people. But Mummy, what's wrong with taking risks?'

'Now don't try to be a saint! And we're late getting home. He can't come with us, you'll just be wasting your time. If you have any big ideas about helping people you'll find thousands of people like this in India, it's a lot worse than in America.'

Guddo put the street people out of her mind and forgot them. In any case, she had not formed any relationship with people here so that she could feel any deep sympathy for them. In India it had been completely natural to help the servants, the maid or washerman if they fell ill. But she felt no responsibility for anyone here, where she still felt like a guest. She had emigrated with a purpose, and her only object was to achieve it. Like other immigrants, she also thought that after she had earned enough money she would probably go back home. She intended to keep earning as long as she felt like it and had the strength for it. When she had enough money to finish the children's education, get them jobs and see them married, then she'd take her earnings and return to India to live in splendour in her house in Chandigarh.

But Pinki warned her, 'When the children find jobs in this country, how can you go back and live all alone in India? All the

70

Indians here keep saying they'll go back, but they never do. Once you get hooked on dollars you won't find it possible to live anywhere else.'

Guddo had not yet been able to think all this through. Her goal was still far away. She would say, 'Why trouble myself thinking about that now? We'll just flow with the stream wherever it takes us. Who knows what lies so far in the future? The most I can do is plan for one or two years ahead.'

All Guddo's planning was solely in terms of her three children; the way she felt these days she couldn't handle anything else. And she realised that since coming to America she was becoming very selfish. In Chandigarh, even though she might not have particularly wanted to, she shared in the sorrows and troubles of her neighbours and her colleagues at the school. But here she felt no commitment at all. For the most part Indians were interested only in things relating to their own advantage or advancement. They took absolutely no action at the social or political level. Nor would they, even in a personal way, do anything to help the weak and needy. True, a few did indeed send money to their families in India – beyond this their world did not extend. Nothing mattered but to work like the very devil and acquire one new convenience or luxury item after another. After all, that was why everybody came to this country! To emerge from the restrictions of class and caste, society and family, to lead a life free of responsibility. Even Guddo's widowhood was no kind of problem, no social transgression here. If she put on a bright colourful sari and wore make-up when she went out, it would not awaken envy or suspicion in the mind of the woman next door.

But on the other hand, the Indians were troubled in the hard lives they led. So every day they were attracted by the eye-catching advertisements and rush to buy the latest fashion, the loudest clothes, radio and television. Perhaps the basis of taste in Asian countries is just this desire to attract attention – to use local designs, colours and models or blend them with other art forms to achieve novel effects to take you by surprise. Everybody mad about something new, looking for the new for the sake of newness but producing nothing but shallow creations without substance and people caught up in superficial forms.

Here an individual's level was judged by clothes and make-up. Guddo bought her clothes only when they had come down in price because they were no longer in style. Even they were almost more than she could afford. Perhaps this was the reason she had found work only as an accounting clerk. Her supervisor was less educated than she, as she had only a BA, but she wore stylish and pretty clothes of good quality – expensive suits and hair done in the latest fashion. The rumour was that she was about to be promoted. This irritated Guddo. No one cared the least about her MA and BT and she had to put up with a woman much younger than herself for her boss.

But by now Guddo was beginning to understand a lot of other things too. Two qualities were very important here if you wanted to get ahead: first of all, smartness, that is, a knack for style, and second, the capacity to push everybody else aside because of an irrepressible hunger to get ahead, in other words, aggressiveness. In this society these two attributes were considered virtues. Anyone who didn't possess them would have to take a beating getting a job, and then on the job too.

So everybody was trying to be part of the race to make themselves smart and aggressive. To become smart there were innumerable shops and schools, dozens of books on the subject were published and sold by the thousands, and some of them became best-sellers. 'How to Talk', 'How do Dress', 'How to Make Friends'. New ready-made formulas every day to acquire every art, and everyone declaring everybody else's formula wrong while offering his own prescription.

Guddo found the same formulas in society and politics. All those big words about freedom and independence which were bandied about, weren't they intended just to prescibe new formulas to trap you? There were restrictions even for dressing, conversing, behaviour. The way the reins of capitalism held every movement, every facet of life in check, even though words like democracy and freedom were on everybody's lips, wasn't this only another way to confine you in another kind of restricting convention?

Guddo was always being asked how literate Indians could put up with the old-fashioned caste and communal divisions which still dominated modern India. But in her eyes the basis of class here was also money and the colour of your skin. Here the WASPS were the Brahmans, the Jews were the Kshatriyas, the Asians were the Vaishyas, the blacks the Shudras – that was how Guddo understood it.

Meantime, Raju was starting to express all sorts of doubts about the Soviet Union. 'Mummy, I've heard that the people there don't get enough to eat. All the money is put into producing nuclear weapons. If anyone speaks out against it they shoot him. It must be a very dangerous country!'

So the influence of American education had fallen on Raju. From the beginning of their schooling children were taught that there was a monster across the ocean called the Soviet Union. One should hate this monster, one must remain ready to destroy it. So was there really a free expression of opinion here? If the government didn't pull the reins, then the leaders of the multinational companies would. They would hold the government fast by their teeth – what else was brainwashing?

While in India there lingered the ghosts of poverty, conservatism, social violence and irrational moral values, here the ghosts of fierce egotism, exaggerated hedonism and loneliness were very much alive, and they numbered in the millions.

Fourteen

Guddo is invoking the deities: 'May Mitra and Varuna be pleased . . . may there be prosperity on the road of wealth . . . may the supreme Lord whose pledge is never broken make us prosper.' The grease of the *ghi* burning in the sacrificial fire makes the air in the room mild and heavy. When the *pandit* tells him to, Raju, silent, rather casual, casts the *ghi* into the fire and comes away. Raju believes in no religion, so why does he take part in this ritual, why doesn't he object? Will this ritual make Raju, Kanika, Tanima, Ashok, Arjun, all of them, apostles of Indian culture? Or does culture mean nothing more than these rituals? Guddo wonders if she herself has understood the essence of it. Or perhaps in the sacrifice of your desires the essence is burned away as well. In carrying on these meaningless ceremonies they'll succeed in being neither Indian nor American. A rootless existence . . . forever the feeling of being outside.

Arjun sits quietly, as though unconcerned. Anima, Tanima, Kanika and Ashok are whispering, the *havan* book set before them. Arjun watches, looking as though he is about to make fun of this whole performance. With him is one of his friends; as soon as their eyes meet he suppresses his rising laughter as though suddenly a cork were jammed into a fountain. Pinki, eyes closed, is murmuring to herself. The corners of the room hum with the fervent voices of Guddo and Gita as they read the scripture. In one corner of the room Guddo's childhood is lurking.

*

74

At home with her mother and father, followers of the Arya Samaj, there was always a *havan*, a ritual fire sacrifice, every Sunday morning. A teacher named Maheshji used to preside. From him Guddo, Gita and their brother Ajit learned Vedic *mantras* and *bhajans*. This was long before Pinki was born. Master Mahesh's relationship with Biji seemed to be that of an adopted brother. While he taught the children he would talk to Biji, sing *bhajans* for her and sometimes listen as well. So long as Master Mahesh was there Biji was very tranquil and seemed stable, but a little while after he left she would begin to shout abuse at the servants or sometimes to beat the children even as she taught them, and went on reproaching their father too. After all the girls were married, he was left in the house to suffer the abuse and insults by himself. In everything she said Biji kept complaining to him and held him responsible for every single thing that went wrong. For each hour of meditation and *bhajans* she spent another in complaints and curses. An odd relationship, her father and mother's! – Guddo often wondered if Biji had ever been physically satisfied. If she had, why would she associate sex with suffering and illness? And that Master Mahesh, who was like her adopted brother ... what went on between them? And that abuse and cursing! But at this point Guddo would realise that she was entering forbidden territory – it was a sin to think such things about her mother.

Afterwards, when they were living in Delhi, there were fewer *havans*. Guddo was already married by then and had her own demanding programme for her growing children. Maheshji still visited two or three times a year; on those occasions Biji would have him stay at their house. For as long as he was with them daily *havans* were performed morning and night, and they were long ones. Otherwise, they would be performed only on Guddo's brothers' birthdays, when the oblations offered were sweet halva, rice pudding and puris. But the ceremony was forbidden on the daughters' birthdays. When once while still a child Guddo asked Biji for a *havan* to be performed on her birthday, Biji said, 'No, no! If we have *havans* on girls' birthdays then afterwards only girls will be born. In the future we must have fewer girls born in this family.'

In these *havans* Guddo found all her cultural standards, her morality and her values. After the ceremony her father would pray, 'Oh Lord! May we all be blessed by this sacrifice. May all our wishes be fulfilled. May all be successful in auspicious works. Give us the spiritual power, Lord, to remain far from falsehood as we bring our desires to fruition. Give us knowledge, give us prosperity, and rain down happiness and peace upon us.'

And Guddo did just this: mustering her spiritual power she set out to search for prosperity and happiness. Surely that wasn't selfish, she thought, for she was only carrying out her religious duty. If a person did what he had to to help his family prosper, that wasn't like lying or manipulating others, was it? So why should one be troubled by doubts?'

*

When more wood is dropped into the *havan* fire, because no *ghi* has been thrown on with it, the flames suddenly flare up. As she leans over the fire, Guddo's eyes are assaulted by a burst of acrid smoke and she feels them burn so much the tears come. As she blinks to open them again her glance encounters a face watching her, a very sad, drawn, somehow wasted face. It is Anima. How she's faded! After only three years of marriage she seems to have aged ten years. Beneath her eyes black circles have appeared. Her complexion has lost all its glow and freshness. When she first came to America how excited she had been, how happily she had said, 'Mummy, how strange it felt to realise that I was going to my own home in America! Everybody asked me if I wasn't awfully worried to be going to a foreign country, and I told them I wasn't because my mother was there so I wasn't really going to a foreign country at all. And then the opportunity to study here! Can there be any place in the world better to study advanced science than America?'

Where is that Anima now?

*

76

Admission to New York University and the scholarship, everything had been arranged beforehand by Guddo. First the MSc, then the PhD. It meant doing the MSc twice, but Anima was excused from certain courses. She was very excited. After five years of hard work she would get her PhD in chemistry, then find a good job in industry. She really felt she had entered into some kind of paradise. She was fascinated by the skyscrapers of Manhattan, buildings so high that if you looked at them up close you could see nothing but their strong foundations. So many of them in glass, how beautiful they looked, buildings made of nothing but glass! And as though this city had never seen darkness, the play of lights all night, so bright that in the skies above the city the stars disappeared in their brilliance.

The atmosphere at Anima's university was completely open and free. Unlike in India, everyone was expected to be self-motivated, and they were free to choose their courses and even their professors. The different departments of the university were scattered through various buildings, interspersed with markets, houses, restaurants, streets and walks which were public thoroughfares – a fascinating complete city in itself, with a park at the very centre. This park was very lively in the evenings, with jazz played on guitars, accordions and drums, and groups of carefree students in jeans and loose shirts, eating hot dogs or drinking soda from cans, holding to each other by waist or shoulder as they hovered and swayed. Within the university grounds were several cafeterias and restaurants offering many different cuisines, fashionable clothing boutiques, and art galleries. For Anima it was all altogether exotic and beguiling. Best of all, she had everything a student could possibly dream of – a convenient laboratory, a vast library and time to study, so all in all she was happier when she came to live with her mother than she'd ever been in her life.

Most surprising of all to her was the atmosphere of sexual freedom at the University. She observed a permissiveness unknown back home, the frank discourse about personal matters, the free interaction of boys and girls, the tolerance for homosexuals. For her own part, she might respond differently now when someone tried to flirt with her but her basic attitude had not changed. If some boy who saw Anima in her colourful embroidered *kurta-pajama* said 'You look terrific!' and tried to make a date, Anima would just smile in return and shake her head. If a student in Chandigarh had said anything like that she would have answered with a scowl. But in neither case did she have any intention of letting it go further.

She did not want to become involved in a physical relationship before completing her studies. Her fears seemed to be much stronger than her desire for satisfaction. She had learned from Guddo to deny her physical needs, and so she wanted to give herself to only one man, a man whom she could love for all her life. Since from childhood on she had been studying in coeducational schools, it was quite natural for her to converse with boys without any shyness. But when there was a possibility of talking that went beyond inconsequential banter she would break off the relationship.

Anima was also becoming aware of herself as an outsider. By now the liberal era of the Sixties, when young people rebelled against authority and wealth, was far behind. The increasing number of poor, unemployed and immigrants had made many aware young people ultraconservative. The decline in job opportunities and the constant arrival of new immigrants had on occasion set these young people against America's policy of welcoming newcomers from abroad. On the personal level they seemed to be friendly with Asians but they felt an antagonism toward the whole society of immigrants. They felt they were being cheated of their jobs and their rights, though there was no question of any organised discrimination.

When during a conversation someone asked Anima, 'Are you a Hindu?' she found it strange. Not at all religious, she had never thought much about it or even regarded herself as a Hindu. She had probably used the word 'Hindu' only when filling out forms in school and college. But how differently people in foreign countries saw you! In India Hindus were in the vast majority and Muslims, Sikhs and Christians were minorities. Anima found it unsettling when she came to America to realise that here she was counted among the minorities too. It was a shock: she would never be in the mainstream, she was always going to feel separate . . .

Fifteen

The Asian students had formed an association of their own which throughout the year presented programmes of music and dance for bringing people together. Among the Indians she met, Anima found a student from Bangladesh, Najma Aziz, particularly intelligent and appealing: about twenty years older than Anima, tall, thin and trim, with an attractive dark complexion and hair wound in a coil on top of her head, like the Buddha's, through which she put a pin set with silver beads. She looked very aristocratic in her crisply starched Dacca sari, and her English was distinguished by an Oxford accent.

She quickly opened up to Anima. 'You couldn't understand the vulnerability of a forty-year-old divorcee,' she said. 'If we become friendly with married men the wives start to worry. Younger women like you don't usually find us to their liking. We're no longer young enough for young people to take an interest in us. And if a middle-aged or elderly man finds me to his taste, well, I'm not inclined to return his interest. So one is left lonely and restless – or sometimes tearful and sobbing.'

Najma, daughter of a highly placed official in the Indian Civil Service, had the style and manners of the Anglicised society of old Calcutta, and she had gone to London to finish her studies. In comparison to her, Anima felt rather insignificant and mediocre. Though they'd both come from India, what a difference there was in their environment, their society and their upbringing!

Najma, who was teaching English literature in a college and doing research in Renaissance literature at the university, had a studio apartment on the campus. It was small but tastefully decorated, with antique Persian silk carpets and a statue of the Buddha on a shelf with books on English literature and philosophy.

When she was twenty, while her father was serving as the Indian ambassador in Paris, she had fallen in love with a young American and went to Calcutta with him to be married. He was an architect who enjoyed wandering around Asian countries with her. Though at first happy in her marriage Najma was aware of a vague lingering sense that she had lost something too. Living like a vagrant, without even a fixed address, she was afraid her marriage could not last.

'John,' she would say, 'do you really love me?'

And he would answer, 'Always the same question! Don't you trust me?'

'Of course I trust you but I'm afraid of losing you.'

'Najma, if a time should ever come when we're tired of being together, oughtn't we to separate?'

She worried constantly because of the difference in their backgrounds and, in fact, never really trusted her husband. Then a clever middle-class Bengali girl took him away from her. Najma had been married in a Muslim ceremony, so she found herself cheated even in her divorce. To get rid of her John had simply to say 'Talak' three times before witnesses, leaving Najma no grounds on which to contest the divorce; nor did she have the strength to fight against the laws of a strange country. She was not even fully aware of her rights. There were no children. Her father advised her to stay in India and finish her education. After all, she was intelligent and she had the advantage of English as her mother tongue.

After her divorce her parents stayed on in India until her father's retirement, when they settled in Bangladesh. Najma then came to the United States and became an American citizen. Apart from her family in Bangladesh she had no one except for a few friends in Calcutta. In the past there had been her husband here in America; now she was here alone.

In time Anima began to get a new perspective on the things

Najma had told her – particularly regarding her relationship with her husband. Surely all the fault could not be John's. Or perhaps in their breakup there was no question of anybody's fault. It was simply a case of necessity brought about because two very good people had not found it possible to go on living together. Najma had told her, 'Maybe John was content to live without ambition. But I kept expecting something more than that and I was always discontented. Always restless to get something more, always complaining, resentful. John couldn't put up with it. That's why he's satisfied with that middle-class Bengali girl.'

Najma wrote poetry in English but had had no success in trying to get it published. Her struggle was still going on. She had been living in New York for some time and knew lots of Indians working in many different fields, officials from the Indian Consulate, Indian artists who had come to study in the Sixties and settled here. The occasions when well-known Indian dancers performed classical dance were moments of great happiness for her. Such artists, she said, deserved a full house, at the least, but even though the theatres they rented were small they were often half empty. But whenever any film actor or singer came, she told Anima scornfully, the biggest theatres in the city were sold out, often on the black market. She also liked to go to concerts of western music as well. She said, 'If I had a child I'd certainly teach him the classical music of this culture. Its tradition is very old and rich but we Indians are not the least curious about it. Many Americans go to India and study its classical music and become accomplished in it, but how many of us Indians who come and live here try to understand and learn about Western music? No, we just study science, we study computers so we can earn good salaries and become prosperous while we go on boasting about our cultural superiority.'

Anima realised that Najma had not yet recovered from the pain of her divorce, but she also recognised Najma's strong sense of her own superiority. All the same, she was impressed by her friend's self-confidence and found their conversations stimulating. One day when they were sitting in the university cafeteria

Najma told her all about her struggle to find a job. As a citizen of this country she had a strong awareness of her rights. She said, 'I'm a citizen of the US so they can't push me around. My English is better than theirs and I speak Hindi and Bengali just as well. What's more, I fight back if any American tries to get the better of me. Even before the interview for my job everyone was dubious about an Asian woman teaching Americans English. But my credentials were the best. Play the game their own way, that's how you succeed.'

Eventually Anima was bored by these monologues of Najma's, so full of self-praise and self-love. But she also saw that Najma was terribly lonely. No matter how attractive her personality on the surface, inside she was hollow and desolate, devoured by loneliness and insecurity.

But then, this was the way to survive in this country: high walls of self-praise and self-love to protect yourself. Any Indian Anima met would let her know in very short order what a successful person he was. Salary, position – that was all they talked about. Even someone doing the most insignificant work would boast about how important his job was. Businessmen talked only in terms of hundreds of thousands, of millions. Nobody admitted that he'd had to apply for a job – the job was always offered. But Anima was shy when it came to talking about herself, she was afraid she'd sound conceited. She was still convinced that a person's real qualities would be revealed at the right moment.

Sixteen

The year passed so quickly that Anima was scarcely aware of it. Classes, study, lab, exams, Najma, and her other friends, Jack and Susan . . . Leisure time had become the most precious thing for her. Even during the summer she took more courses, and along with that, did tutoring.

Meantime, Guddo was now troubled by quite different worries. She was opposed to delaying Anima's marriage until she had finished her education. In only four more years Anima would be twenty-six. A girl ought to be married by twenty-three at the latest. Guddo herself had been only twenty. She was convinced that if they put it off any longer they wouldn't find a suitable bridegroom.

Guddo began to study the matrimonial advertisements in the local Indian newspapers. 'Brahman boy, four-figure salary, looking for beautiful, homey girl.' Or: 'Doctor, 33, looking for bride – must be a doctor, caste no bar.' Then Guddo herself started placing ads.

But Anima was not ready to get married. She did not want to become involved with marital problems until she had at least finished her studies. Every other day she would meet new people at the University. When she had the time, after class she would go somewhere or other for coffee with Jane, Susan, and Najma.

Susan said, 'I'm not the marrying kind.'

'What do you mean?' Anima asked her. 'Aren't you ever going to get married?'

'No, never!'

'Then you plan to be a spinster?'

'Shame on you, using such out-of-date language.'

'But how can a woman be fulfilled without having children?'

'Well if you want so much to be a mother, you don't have to get married for that. I think that if at some stage in my life I have to become a mother to be fulfilled, well, I'll certainly have a child.'

'Without marriage?'

'Why not? What's the connection between marriage and children? Of course, to bring them up you have to have money – but not a husband.'

With the values she had learned from her mother, Anima found these ideas shocking. She could not even conceive of a physical relationship before marriage, and to become a mother without a husband was nothing less than suicide.

But when she thought about it Anima wanted to marry only a man who would let her maintain her relationship with Guddo. That was one's responsibility toward a widowed mother. On the other hand, with her advanced education the idea of an arranged marriage was repugnant to her. But since she had no male friends she wanted to marry, might her mother's way not be reasonable? Guddo might even find a man for her she would like.

For her part, Guddo had one condition: her son-in-law must be a doctor, so that Anima could live in comfort, even luxury. Unlike her mother, Anima should never have to worry about money for her daily needs. Doctors earned good salaries, so she could live happily, whether she herself earned any money or not – that was up to her.

But nothing was being settled, so Guddo wrote to her brother and his wife in Delhi to advertise for a doctor in the newspaper matrimonials and pick out some who might be suitable for Anima. Then they'd go back to India next year and arrange a marriage with the one Anima liked most.

An opportunity to marry a beautiful, educated girl and along with that the chance to go to America! So of course Guddo's brother Ajit received a great number of interesting replies to the advertisement and began to look over the most promising candidates.

Guddo, in the meantime, was kept busy making elaborate dinners for prospective bridegrooms, their parents or any relatives who might be living in the city. Anima was furious. 'Are you always going to keep up these Indian customs here?' she protested. 'What's the point of all this hard work and hospitality? Are these people coming here looking for a bride or a free meal? Even in New York you're still trapped in all those useless customs. I really hate it! You don't even realise how obsessed you've become over getting me married. I won't get married this way, it's just too ridiculous and humiliating.'

Her friend Jane said, 'How can modern Indian girls like you accept a husband picked out by your parents? The fundamental thing in marriage is the mutual attraction of the man and woman and their wish to live together. Without this how is the relationship possible?'

Anima realised that for Indians there was no question of a marriage based on mutual attraction. The attraction of man and woman, they thought, was always natural and spontaneous, so if everything else – that is, family, rank, general appearance – was all right, the rest would follow – and if it didn't, well, too bad, that was fate. But even without realising it Anima sought to justify every Indian custom to her American friends by logic.

'We have to meet our husband by some means or other, Jane, whether our parents bring us together or some other way. I'm certainly not going to marry somebody just on the basis of having a look at him. We'll have to meet several times, talk together, and then I'll decide. You people think of an arranged marriage as something fiendish, but it's nothing at all like that.'

Still, she was getting more and more troubled and irritated by the whole process of looking and being looked at. She finally said to Guddo:

'Mother, how could anyone ever get married that way? I think it's ridiculous! You sent me off to the movies with that fellow from New Jersey – how could I refuse in front of everyone? I didn't know the least thing about him, I felt nervous and self-conscious. Do you think we could even have a decent conversation in those conditions? He said to me, "Do you have any idea of what kind of man you want to marry?" What a stupid question! What does "idea" mean? I'll marry a man I like. I'm not going to formulate any "ideas" and try to fit somebody into them afterwards. So we didn't say a word to one another the whole time we were at the movies. If we spoke, it was just to impress one another. Or pry. And while you're trying to impress somebody what's really important just gets lost in the shuffle.

'You remember that boy from Long Island? He told me, "I've got lots of girlfriends but for a bride I insist on an Indian girl because she'll know how to respect a husband. I don't like the feminist attitude these American girls have. If you're like that too, then say so." Please, mother, I want to stop this nonsense!'

Guddo assured her that this was only a temporary phase. She herself had had to go through it. In the beginning she hadn't particularly liked her husband because he wasn't six feet tall but of average height and looks. But later, when she realised what a good, intelligent and loving husband she had found, she felt that this way of marriage was not wrong.

Gita's experience had been different. She was attracted to one of her colleagues, but Biji and her father couldn't wait for him to be settled in his career. So she was married to someone else against her will, and as a result, like a sacrificial goat, always wore an expression of helplessness and misery. At her in-laws' she always seemed suppressed and silent. Nobody could recognise her as the Gita who in the past would raise a storm at the slightest provocation. She had certainly raised a storm in opposition to this marriage, but then, in the face of her parents' pressure, along with that of the groom's family, she was forced to agree to it.

But in America she had begun to regain her confidence and from time to time was even seen to smile. Since coming to New York, even in the midst of money troubles and her other problems, Gita had found something that belonged to her alone: herself, her home, her children. From so much struggling with every kind of hardship she had learned to do battle in a way that was highly disciplined, tough and calculating too. She did not fight back but accepted, and her acceptance was silent.

The one who fought back was Pinki. There was a kind of furious energy in her that would not let her leave anything alone once it had caught her imagination, even when it came to marrying Satinder. Her father had forbidden it, for there was no telling when the boy would go to America and finish his education and they couldn't keep an unmarried daughter at home so long. But Pinki got a job as a secretary so she wouldn't be idle at home, reminding her parents that she wasn't married. Anyway, she was the youngest, so it wasn't so urgent to marry her off. Besides, her parents' remorse over marrying Gita so quickly still troubled them. Pinki had to wait a full four years after getting her BA for Satinder.

'Well, marriage is a gamble' – so Guddo would tell Anima. 'If it jells, fine, otherwise the matter of fulfilment remains unsettled. Whether it's a love match or an arranged marriage, the risk is the same. Anyway, one has to marry, it's the only true goal for a woman. If we don't get our children married we're shirking our duty to them. Without marrying you can't really get launched in life, you've just missed the boat!'

Guddo wanted to see Anima safely settled in the kind of situation where she herself could control her destiny. Or if not she, then someone else: only then would Guddo's responsibility come to an end.

About this time a letter came from Tanima. 'Mummy, Anima must have told you all about it . . . Last week I went to meet Anuj's parents. They're fine people, and they said we could be married as soon as we finish our MBBS and afterwards I should come to America. They want the wedding to be in India. But Anuj doesn't want to come to America. He's an only child, you know. But I'm not agreeing to that.

'What I would like, Mummy, is for us to do our residency and specialisation in the US, then come back to Chandigarh and open a clinic in Daddy's name. How would you feel about turning our house in Chandigarh into a nursing home? You would be our administrative manager and take care of all the accounting. We'd give free medical treatment to the poor and make the rich pay through the nose!'

Guddo too had dreamt of something like this – 'Prem Nursing Home'. She liked the ring of that name. She would get rid of her tenants and establish it in her own house. Her husband had himself laid the foundation stone of that house. Thousands of miles away, Guddo began to picture it in her imagination: the clean bright rooms, Tanima and a young man in white gowns, the patients lying on beds made up with clean white sheets, a nurse standing by with medicine and injections on a tray . . . Then, without her being aware of it, this world of the future suddenly began to turn back in time, into the past . . . that unconscious person lying in the hospital bed – she recognised his face . . . long needles kept piercing him and drawing out blood . . . tests . . . no one could say how many tests or what they were called . . . Guddo felt as though someone were drawing out her own blood, her very breath. The medicine couldn't be found in India, they must try in London. But by the time the medicine arrived from London her husband's soul had taken flight. Guddo's mind and body were numb, she felt paralysed. When her tears flowed it was as though they hadn't stopped for years.

Tanima was close to ten when Prem died. She kept asking, 'Why did Daddy die?' She had heard that word but still had no very clear idea of what it meant. Guddo explained that because the proper medicine wasn't available in India he could not be saved. So right then Tanima said, 'I'm going to be a great doctor and scientist. Then I'll open up a clinic in Chandigarh.' Guddo cried for hours and hours. Her little girl's resolve had remained exactly the same all these years, and to carry it out she had found a companion. How lucky she was today!

Now Guddo felt it was even more urgent to see Anima married. She was the elder, she should be married first, otherwise people, for no good reason, would begin to say there was something wrong with her. With the greatest deliberation Guddo planned her strategy. As soon as Tanima had taken her exams they would go to India and find a fine husband for Anima from among the best proposals Ajit had received. Afterwards Tanima's wedding could take place – or possibly the two girls' weddings simultaneously.

They could manage quite well with Anima's scholarship and Guddo's salary, and even Raju's school fees were no longer a problem. All the necessary items had already been bought: television, radio, tape recorder, Corning ware, sofa, table lamps, and the like. Guddo had begun some time before to buy and store saris and other things for the two weddings. The shops were not far away. Saris, electric appliances, gifts for the relatives – every Saturday and Sunday Guddo was busy with shopping. And these days she was even able to put away some savings.

Then she received another letter from Tanima. 'I'm starting to miss you terribly. A while back I was quite ill. The principal told me that if I can get an internship in some hospital in America she'll combine the December break with some other time off and let me take three months' leave. Now I have to do an internship here too. Please find out if there's anything there. I haven't been home for so many years. It won't be the same when I come home after I'm married.'

Guddo wondered if she should talk to Dr Juneja about Tanima. She was beginning to be very dependent on Dr Juneja. Since her own daughter was to be a doctor he had taken an even greater interest in her children. He told Guddo that his nephew was studying medicine too and he wanted to marry only a woman who was also a doctor. 'We should bring him and Tanima together,' he said. 'I think they should make an excellent match.' Only – Tanima had already made her own match. But for the moment Guddo decided not to tell Dr Juneja about that. If not Tanima, then she would introduce him to Anima – for when Anima got her PhD she would be a doctor too.

Nowadays Guddo could do nothing without Dr Juneja's advice. Minor domestic problems, illness or fear of illness – he was indispensable for everything. She spoke to him about Tanima. He told her that it was becoming impossible for doctors coming from abroad to find a residency here. In the big cities particularly there was an oversupply and in hospitals salaries were not being raised but reduced. All the same, he was able to arrange an internship for Tanima in his hospital and said he would try his best to find a residency for her. 'For she's like my own daughter, isn't she, my dear?'

When Tanima finally came to New York and began her internship everyone was pleased with her work. Dr Juneja said to her, 'Probably I shouldn't tell you this yet but your residency here is definite. You can start your work next year.'

Tanima could hardly believe it. Overcome with happiness, she could only say to Juneja, 'Thank you, thank you so much!'

A few days later she told him about her fiancé in India.

Dr Juneja was taken completely by surprise.

'Oh yes,' she went on, 'Mummy's agreed to our marriage. Our engagement isn't official yet, but it's all settled. Do you think you could do something for him? We'll be coming over right after the wedding.'

Juneja did not have the heart to disappoint her. In any case, he had promised Guddo. There was nothing he could do about her unfortunate decision to marry but he couldn't go back on his word. Tanima would get her appointment, but as for her fiancé . . .

'Tanima, I can't say anything at all right now, but I'll certainly try.'

'Oh please, I'll be so grateful to you!'

The pleading expression in Tanima's bright eyes touched a responsive chord in Juneja. Later on he said to Guddo, 'So many people ask me to give them jobs and I turn them all down. Conditions are bad. If I appoint an Indian I'll risk damaging my reputation. But – I don't know why! – I can never manage to say no to you.'

Her eyes filled with gratitude, Guddo said, 'I have complete confidence in you, and nobody else.'

Still, whenever she thought about Juneja, Guddo was troubled by many questions. Did she keep up her affair with him only to find jobs for her children or getting them settled? Wasn't this the same as selling herself? Or was it rather that she really liked him so much that she looked for any excuse at all to be with him? And Juneja! Was he just as attached to her? Or was she merely

91

something to satisfy his physical needs? But he had a wife for that sort of thing. Guddo felt a shiver down her spine.

In this relationship they made no promises. Juneja had never yet used the word 'love'. Perhaps he reserved it for his wife alone. For her part, she had never become free of the shadow of her husband. Maybe something of that image was reflected in Juneja, which would explain why she had so easily come to put her trust in him and become so devoted to him. But what kind of unspoken, unwritten agreement was this? Parallel lives suddenly brought close together by some incident, some problem, some party or celebration, then the two of them cut apart, each of them lost in his own life. Sometimes she would feel restless with her desire for him, then, distressed, she'd begin to try to break off. Her Arya Samaj moral standards would turn her away from him, so she was constantly at war with herself. She had been weak and now her soul was enslaved by another man . . . and a man who had to belong to someone else . . . These fires . . . fires turning her to ash . . . Where was Agni, that purifying god? Agni had burned all the demons to ash, hadn't he? If he could burn this demon of her desires she would be pure again . . .

Juneja's hands were gently caressing her temples. Startled, Guddo moved away and said, 'Please, not this . . .'

'What's happening to you?' Juneja's eyes were still caressing her.

As she was sitting down Guddo said suddenly, 'You and I don't have any real relationship.'

'What do you mean? What relationship could be more real than this?'

'We can never marry. I'm a widow, I'm alone – does that make you feel sorry for me?'

'Why do you insist on seeing it that way? Think of all the two of us share together, the way we're always longing for one another's company, talking for hours, facing our troubles together – isn't this a relationship? How lonely we feel, living abroad! Don't we need this relationship to go on living? Doesn't this mean anything at all to you?'

Guddo felt she was beginning to understand something. 'Of

course – but for how long? How can this relationship continue? Don't you feel the least bit guilty about Ramna?'

Juneja was silent for a moment; then he said, emphasising each word, 'I don't feel guilty. These two relationships are completely separate. They're both important to me. You can't take Ramna's place, nor can Ramna take yours. You're my friend. Love is the basis for frienship too. Look at it that way and you can call it love.'

Guddo was staring at Juneja. Then, mustering her courage, she said, 'You must realise, there's a battle going on inside me all the time. Sometimes I feel like giving myself to you completely . . . that New Year's Eve . . . But then something like a feeling of guilt rises up in me – how could I let it happen like that? What I want to tell you today is that you must never let it happen again.'

'But what we do is entirely natural. When you take someone into your heart, the body is nothing more than a manifestation of the same feeling.'

'Maybe you're right. But it troubles me a great deal.'

'Why are you denying your natural needs? Are you afraid of something?'

Guddo sighed. 'I'm not afraid of anything outside myself, but inside me everything seems to be falling apart. I feel that to hold myself together, to keep strong and complete, I simply have to avoid any physical contact with a man. What I'm saying must sound strange to you. But I just feel that being close to a man makes me weak, dependent. And alone. While you can just go back to your family. What can such a relationship mean? For me, only depression, worry, feelings of guilt – and this leads to futile anxiety and insecurity in my children's lives. I'm a mother, I've got to keep myself solid as the ground under my feet, the ground that gives life to everything and makes it mean something . . .'

Guddo had spoken with passion. With unaccustomed emotion Juneja embraced her. Guddo began to sob.

'I'm very weak,' she said. 'Completely alone and helpless. I don't know how I'm going to get through the rest of my life . . .'

Juneja gently patted her cheeks. He said, 'But you're Uma,

and that means you have the strength of Shakti. Shakti's greater than all the other gods and goddesses. Remember, even Ram had to worship Shakti with a sacrifice before he could defeat Ravan. You're truly a mother, you give life, how can you say you're weak?'

Guddo fixed her eyes on Juneja. 'You're forgetting, Uma also had to burn to ash in Daksha's sacrifice.'

Smiling rather weakly, Juneja said, 'That was Sati, but you're burning up in a sacrificial fire of self-denial and inhibition.'

Guddo put her fingers on his lips to hush him. She said, 'No, no . . . it's a sacrifice for well-being. For everybody's well-being.'

Seventeen

Just as she had planned, Guddo returned to India to arrange marriages for both her daughters. At the airport, the moment she stepped from the plane, a familiar smell in the air, the expanse of blue sky, the feel of the sunlight on her body, everything thrilled her through and through. Then the immigration queue, waiting for the baggage, and as soon as she came out of the airport, the awareness of crowds and dirt. She had completely forgotten about Indian dust and dirt.

Her mother, her brothers and their wives, the nephews and nieces – everybody came to the airport. Raju and Anima were with Guddo, while Tanima had returned a few months earlier, after finishing her internship and was now in Ludhiana, preparing for her last exam.

As she looked at the children Guddo became aware of how much time had gone by. She had been away five whole years. Talking, endless talking, endless tea, advice about the weddings – this was how she passed the first few days. Both brothers were there to help, interviewing young men for Anima every day. They were doing everything in a great rush. Guddo had taken five weeks leave from the bank, and during this time she was going to have to see to Tanima's formal engagement and wedding, choosing a boy for Anima and arranging her betrothal and wedding.

Guddo went to Phagvara to meet Tanima's future in-laws. Tanima and Anuj had come there straight from Ludhiana. Guddo found Anuj good-looking, well-mannered and promising – Tanima ought to be happy. The two young people were

95

constantly teasing one another. Guddo said, 'You two still have a lot of growing-up to do,' but all the same she liked their playfulness. Anuj's family was financially solid. They were educated people and very pleased with Tanima. They also agreed that the wedding should be in Chandigarh, where Guddo could take charge of everything. She had spent lavishly, borrowing where she could, on the assumption that with her salary in America she would have no difficulty repaying the loans. Her relatives her brothers, lawyers, Mr Batra, everybody was in attendance, ready to help her with all the arrangements. At the *shagun*, offered by the bride's family, Guddo gave thirty-one platters of sweets and fruit, along with an envelope containing one hundred and one rupees to each of the relatives, five hundred and one to the father-in-law, a sari and gold chain to the mother-in-law, and a ring, a new suit and a thousand rupees to the groom.

But when has a wedding ever gone off without a hitch, complaints or tensions? Someone sneered that in their family it was the custom to present a whole set of gold jewelry. Guddo was furious. Carping like this after all she had done! If she had stayed on in India she would never have been able to do so much. For a moment Guddo was glad she lived far away from her whole community.

In the evening, when the groom's party came over to her house for the *chunni* and *mehndi* ceremonies, Guddo, in her turn, could not resist calculating what everything was worth. The gold set was indeed very heavy. Only – had they really given it or was it just put out for show? But they had only the one son, so she felt they ought to offer real gold. On the other hand, at home they still had two daughters to marry, so who could tell. Before leaving India, Guddo said to Tanima, 'Don't leave that gold jewelry your mother-in-law gave you with her when you come to America. Bring everything with you and I'll rent a vault for you in New York.'

But Tanima's mother-in-law not only kept the gifts but even the jewelry Guddo had given her daughter because, as she said, it would only get lost in a foreign country, so everything would be safer with her.

With Tanima settled, Guddo turned her attention to Anima. She had only ten days before she was to return, but all Anima's shopping had already been done along with her sister's.

The families of three or four boys were eager for the marriage. Ajit and Ramya, his wife, were particularly impressed with one of the young men. Anima had met him three times and seemed to like him, but she said he was not as sophisticated as she wanted. She couldn't make up her mind. Ramya said, 'You've come from America so you chatter about sophistication! But this is the way boys are in India. When he goes to America he'll get sophistication.'

Her aunt and uncle, her grandmother, everybody said how good-looking he was, how tall, and he was a doctor with an excellent family, so why all this shilly-shallying?

Anima was weary with thinking about it. She couldn't figure out what she ought to do. If she just went back, then all the planning, all the running around her mother, uncle and aunt had done, the whole trip to India, everything would be wasted. She had considered so many boys, not just here but in America too. In an arranged marriage love didn't blossom at first sight, that was possible only when you got to know someone. And if you kept score in every department, then by comparison with the others Rakesh turned out to be a fine boy. But of course in America she had become accustomed to American speech and American ways so she naturally found him somewhat lacking. Still, he was acceptable in every way, and he was so good-hearted too. And he'd told everybody again and again how much he liked her. So finally Anima said yes. After that, a quick engagement ceremony and a quicker wedding. Within five days the bridegroom's party arrived. Guddo had made arrangements for the banquet at Chandigarh's best hotel. She had to borrow more money, but nobody hesitated to lend her what she needed because they were eager to have their rupees repaid in dollars. Especially those who were still dreaming of going to America.

Everyone said, 'These two weddings have been like a miracle!

What splendid arrangements! What hospitality she showed the groom's party! How clever Guddo is! And how smart she's become by going to America. She was so efficient organising everything in a hurry. She ran the whole family ragged getting those two girls married but she managed everything perfectly all by herself.' Biji said wearily, 'Well now, we don't have to worry about her two daughters any more. As it is, Ajit and Umesh have been working at it a whole year. All *she* did was write a letter from over there – do this, do that! If her brothers hadn't made all the preparations, nothing would have come of it.'

As the new term was about to begin at Anima's university two weeks after the wedding, Anima went with Rakesh to spend the few days till then with his parents in Bhopal.

Raju was constantly busy playing games with his friends or cousins, football or monopoly, keeping at them for hours, not even remembering to eat. Guddo, because she was so caught up in the things she had to do, often forgot to call him in for his meals. But when he felt really hungry and asked for food, he would polish off one dish after another. For the first time in years Guddo heard real spontaneous laughter coming from him, and when he spoke to her there was eagerness and pleasure in his voice such as she had never heard before.

'Mummy, Pintu says he's never even seen a computer, but I've got a computer at school.'

'Go on now,' Guddo would say so her brother's son would not feel hurt, 'he's seen lots of other things you haven't, remember.'

Encouraged, Pintu would say, 'Yes, Auntie, he says he's never even seen a peacock.'

And the jokes and teasing and games would start up again.

Eighteen

Guddo had scarcely finished with all the activities connected with the two weddings when it was time for her to return to New York. Although she felt relieved to see both daughters married, she still had problems. For one thing, as soon as she got back she would have to begin applying for the green cards necessary for bringing her sons-in-law to America.

With mingled tears and laughter she made her farewells to Biji, her brothers and daughters and their new in-laws. How many new relations she had suddenly acquired! She hadn't even time to get to know them, but no matter, if only they could all be happy in their own homes. She comforted herself by reciting the Gayatri *mantra*, which would make everything turn out all right. They were all going to come to her in America anyway. When Tanima burst into tears as she was setting out for her husband's home, her mother-in-law said, 'But we're the ones who should be crying! It's our son who's going to be leaving us. This visit is just a part of the ceremony.'

Nevertheless, Guddo trembled with foreboding.

By the time Anima was back at her university it was as though she had completely forgotten that she was married. She had spent ten days in Rakesh's home, mostly in the company of the family members. When she was alone with Rakesh at night he would suffocate her with kisses and hot, bone-crushing embraces, in which she experienced both pleasure and pain. She would have preferred someone who could express his love with gentle

99

caresses. And yet, though in Rakesh's uncontrollable passion there was urgency, there was impatience, there were shocks, but Anima's physical hunger remained somehow unsatisfied. Still, whatever pleasure she got from this passionate and urgent loving, she tried to absorb completely in herself. Once back in America she remembered Rakesh's love only as a rather pleasing episode, and her old surroundings at the university began to provoke some doubts. Had she done the right thing in marrying? She kept wondering and trying to reassure herself. Sometimes she would be distressed, thinking she had foolishly rushed into it, until she shoved all her worries aside, remembering that it would be at least a year before he came. Then they would see. And, immersing herself in her work, she would forget about the whole upsetting experience.

Anima had a temperament like Guddo's, for it was Guddo who had moulded her. Whatever happened, both of them would adjust. And Rakesh had said too, 'Anni, as soon as you looked at me it felt good. I decided on the spot that I'd marry this girl.'

Anima felt an acute longing to repeat those moments. She would dream of herself and Rakesh at Niagara Falls, drenched in the spray, clinging to one another, held tight against his body, gazing in wonderment at the far-flung expanses and bright cliffs of the Grand Canyon, or whirling high on the rides at Disneyland. Many were the nets of the imagination which Anima cast out and gathered in. Now she would never again feel alone, the two would always be together as they moved on to better and better places. As soon as she finished her PhD she would find a good position in industry. And since Rakesh was a doctor they would never want for money. They'd build a beautiful house which she would decorate to perfection.

Very quickly the mice of reality began to nibble away at her net of dreams. Rakesh wouldn't have a job the moment he got to New York, who could say how long it would take? Anima's scholarship wasn't big enough for them to have their own place. Then Tanima and Anuj would be coming. Until Tanima got her residency next year they would all have to live in that tiny apartment.

The same worry was tormenting Guddo even more than Anima. How were they going to arrange things when both sons-in-law were there? Guddo and Anima made a thorough study of the whole situation and drew their conclusions.

First of all: in India the daughter-in-law traditionally goes to live with her husband's family. Whatever conditions may be like there, she adjusts. In this case, the husbands would be coming to live with their in-laws, so they would have to adjust to conditions as best they could.

Next: after getting the sons-in-laws their green cards (which on Guddo's part constituted the most important part of the dowries), in principle the brides' family could not be expected to be responsible for giving them a home and finding jobs for them as well. They should be grateful for marrying girls who were not only beautiful, educated and capable of earning, but were even taking the responsibility of finding them jobs, offering them a roof over their heads and feeding them. This was surely no less generous than giving them the opportunity to come to America. Therefore there could be no objection to finding some kind of compromise.

Guddo had incurred so many debts that it was out of the question for her to think of moving to a bigger apartment.

It was decided that Rakesh and Anima would have Raju's room, Tanima and Anuj Guddo's room, and Raju and Guddo would sleep in the living room.

From then on Raju's life was like that of a passive onlooker. He watched everything and took part in nothing. In the beginning, when he first came to America, he was neither young enough to make a fuss about anything nor old enough to remain unconcerned. At Halloween when children put on costumes and joined in groups to go from house to house he realised that he belonged to no group of his own. At Christmas, when other children talked about their gifts and decorating the trees, again he felt that he was left out of the celebration. When he went with his mother to look at the city decorations, looking was all there was. Guddo said that Christmas trees were expensive and as Christmas wasn't their festival why waste money and work on it?

Because the day before Christmas the trees were sold very cheap, on one occasion Guddo bought one to satisfy Raju. But since there was no time to decorate it properly, they made do by hanging a string of electric lights and some New Years cards on the branches – a make-shift arrangement that gave Raju no pleasure; on the contrary, he felt ashamed.

His sisters' weddings had brought a refreshing rainy season into Raju's withered life. Then, coming home, the same old routine began again. Anima at the university, Mummy at the bank, himself in school. After school he would watch television, read some book, and do his homework to get ready for the next day. He had never found a way to take an active part in any social activity or to have any fun. His grades were good, and this was enough to relieve Guddo of her worries, for at first her only real concern was with his grades; if they were good he'd be accepted by some first-rate college.

But meantime, she began to observe that Raju was becoming very self-sufficient and self-involved, as though he had no need of anybody else. Whether she came home late or early, whether Anima was at home or at the lab until midnight, seemed not to conern him at all. He was beginning to seem like a stranger in his own house. Guddo was frightened. In the smoke of the sacrificial fire fearsome figures began to take shapes, monstrous faces, ugly creatures casting lumps of flesh into the flames . . . hideous faces like the demons attacking Ram and Lakshman as they protected Vishvamitra's sacrifice. Thick tangled locks, long fangs, tongues flickering and darting out of their mouths, crude ravening hunger in their eyes – so Guddo imagined them. But maybe this was only because she had seen them on television, or possibly they were the faces in Raju's comic books, which were just as frightening, just as hideous.

She would say to Raju, 'Why are you so wrapped up in yourself? Have you found a girlfriend?'

And somewhere deep in her mind Guddo was aware of what it meant for Raju not to have a father. A teenage boy establishes a line of communication with his father of a kind he can't have with his mother. While Guddo had always felt close to her

102

daughters, with Raju she was embarrassed where personal and sexual matters were concerned. Now she felt that Raju was drawing even further away from her. In his world filled with the passive violence of science fiction, comic books, television and video games there was nothing to interest Guddo, nothing she could understand. So she was afraid that Raju would become a complete stranger. Violence on television in its cruellest and ugliest forms offered Raju his daily companionship.

Annoyed, she said, 'Why do you keep watching it, Raju, what kind of pleasure is there in all this fighting and bloodshed? It's going to have a harmful effect on you.'

'All the boys here watch it, why shouldn't I?'

'Why don't you play with your friends outside? Why do you play alone at home? What are those cards you've got there?'

'Nothing, just baseball cards.'

'Aren't you bored playing by yourself?'

'Please, Mummy, don't interrupt my game. I play with my friends when I'm at school.'

'Now look, put that aside and talk to me.'

With his eyes still glued on his game he said, 'What am I supposed to say?'

Angry, Guddo said, 'What's happening to you, Raju?'

'Why are you getting upset over nothing?' Said carelessly.

'Aren't you happy here?'

'Sure. When are we going back to India again?'

Guddo was startled. Then, to give him some kind of answer, she said, 'We're going to have our India right here when Anuj and Rakesh and Tanima come over.'

Although mother and son rarely had much to say to one another, each found some serenity in the other's presence, and Anima rarely ruffled the general calm. But when Tanima and the sons-in-law arrived there were five adults living together with him in this tiny apartment. On the surface, new and delicate relationships, but for Raju peculiarly upsetting, a violent storm in the lake of his life. When he was told to vacate his room and sleep in the living room he felt that his own private world was being invaded.

'Mother, how can I study? They'll be disturbing me all the time. Can't I at least stay in my own room?'

Raju's advice was not asked for in the plans Guddo and Anima made. Guddo, who until now had been constantly busy with seeing to Raju's meals and other needs, was now completely taken up with providing hospitality for her sons-in-law. Even Raju was made to run errands time and again for their convenience, whether to travel to the airport to collect their luggage or to go out and shop for them. Raju found this crowded and tumultuous household unnatural, no longer his own. As the time for his final exams approached he became very worried and said to Guddo:

'First you say you want me to get into an ivy league university, then the next thing you do is take my room away from me. I can't find any peace in this house so how can I study?'

Guddo was worried now too but could see no solution. Neither of the sons-in-law had a job, nor had Tanima yet found her residency. The sons-in-law thought of very little but enjoying their pleasures as newly-weds. Guddo's financial woes were far beyond their capacity to grasp. Their connection with dollars was purely nominal, so Guddo was responsible for paying everything, even their smallest pocket expenses. Fortunately, Anima was getting a scholarship, otherwise with nothing but Guddo's salary it would have been difficult even to buy their food. Either Rakesh or Anuj at one time or another would be wanting to call up their families in India. Guddo was furious at having to pay their telephone bills – she who in order to save money would never telephone anyone there, and here they were, squandering her dollars. Anyway, what was the need of talking so long? At the same time they had begun the process of looking for a job, but that didn't decrease their expenses in the least.

And then, to make her situation even more miserable, the sons-in-law insisted on Indian food. She would get up at five in the morning to make parathas and the like and, for lunch, vegetables and dal, before she went to the office. Then she would have to make dinner when she returned. Tanima was completely unaccustomed to housework, and she had never learned to cook anything at all. Only Anima, after working in the lab all day, might help a little in the evenings. All the while, the two young men would sit around like special guests. It never even occurred to them that they might take it upon themselves to share in the housework, and everyone else was too embarrassed to say anything about it. It was wearing Guddo out. When several weeks went by like this she finally became really angry. She had somehow ended up becoming the servant for everyone in the household. She summoned her daughters and explained the situation once and for all:

'If you two don't take a stand about making them help with the housework, how will your husbands learn to be of any use? Somehow or other you have to get them to enjoy helping out.' To her doctor daughter Tanima she said, 'Look, you and your husband are absolutely equal. You're just as educated and just as competent as Anuj. There's not the slightest reason for you to let him lounge at his ease while you feed him chapatis. The two of you should work together. From now on you mustn't encourage his bad habits. Otherwise you'll end up wearing yourself out slaving for him and he'll just take it for granted.'

Then, after a pause, she said, 'A woman is only as important as she claims to be.'

When Tanima asked Anuj to help her mother with the work he was ready and willing. Now he was always asking things like: 'Shall I take this rubbish out? Let me put the dishes in the sink. I've learned how to make chicken curry – let me make it for you?' But Rakesh had the typical Indian son-in-law's arrogance. He would say, 'I didn't get married so I could cook dinner in my wife's house. A man has to be mindful of his honour.'

Months went by in this way. Raju, worried about his exams, fretted and complained more than ever. Guddo said to Anima, 'He simply can't study properly in the living room. Can't you and Rakesh give him your room?'

That same day Anima and Rakesh moved into the living room. One solution and a new problem: at five in the morning Guddo would have to go through the living room to reach the kitchen to make breakfast. Hearing the noises in the kitchen, Rakesh was irritated. 'Are we going to have our sleep spoiled every morning by that racket? If somebody has to get up early to study why can't he sleep here in the living room? But little Brother-in-law Sahib is the boss here, I guess. Don't we count for anything in this house? Ask him what's wrong with the living room. He doesn't have a wife to sleep with, does he?'

Then each of the sisters began to quarrel about the other's husband. Tanima would say to Anima, 'Why don't you tell your lord and master to shake himself up and get a move on? All he does is sit around the house the whole day doing nothing.'

'And who does Anuj think he is? He's not cooking any meals for us, is he? I'd rather not argue with Rakesh about this now. At least he does keep doing something or other to find himself a job. After all, these days that's his first priority. I don't think you have any right to criticise my husband.'

The house was now divided into two opposing camps.

Nineteen

Anuj and Tanima were now ready to take their state qualifying exams. For the moment Rakesh, who felt he needed more time to study, decided to postpone his. Tanima said, 'Well, if he doesn't want to now and won't be getting his residency for a while why can't he get a temporary job? That way at least he'd have some kind of income.'

Guddo agreed. 'Nanda's husband couldn't begin work as a doctor the moment he came over so for some time he worked as a lab technician in a hospital. And that's where he got his residency as soon as a vacancy came up. People here don't see anything wrong with that. A man isn't made small by taking a small job.'

Rakesh lost his temper when he heard this. From his point of view he'd been insulted. 'Who the hell do they think they are, telling me what to do? Because they've fed me for a little while they think they can order me around. I'm a son-in-law too, don't I have any rights?'

Inside he was boiling. 'Until I get the work I've trained for I'm not going to take some job that's beneath me. If I did who knows if I'd ever have a chance to get ahead. And these people would never respect me.'

At times, feeling depressed and desperate, he would say to Anima, 'I'm going back to India. If I'd known how hard it is to get a residency here I never would have come.' Anima was troubled; from the way he spoke she feared he really would go back. Maybe he didn't care for her at all but had come in the first place only to look for a job with a good American salary. His face seemed permanently overcast with discontent and frustration,

107

and she realised that he was venting all his anger on her. One day when she came home late from the university he went into a rage.

'You knew I was hanging around the house just waiting for you and still you come home late. This bloody country of yours is really weird – the husband waits at home while the wife goes out gallivanting.'

He was also irritated by her concern for her family. 'All you ever think about is your mother and brother and sister,' he said, 'you don't have the slightest consideration for me.'

This hurt Anima most of all.

Rakesh felt as though fate had played a terrible trick on him. Because of America he had got himself locked up like a prisoner in this gloomy, shabby little apartment that was no better than a cage. The other birds in this cage were suffocating too for want of the sky and starting to peck at one another in their despair. Thinking he would get rich when he came to America, he found instead that there was no hope of his earning anything at all. He grew weary of sending out applications and being rejected every time. Worse, he learned that he was expected to share in the housework and do the shopping. As though his Memsahib had not got married but simply sent to India for a servant.

Guddo was filled with regret and misgiving. Was she then responsible for all this? What she had believed would be the road to liberation was now blocked by even more obstacles. She had to feed and clothe her sons-in-law and at the same time put up with their criticism and complaints. She kept her anger locked inside her as best she could and remained outwardly compliant. Her daughters' happiness was at stake, it was up to her to make things work out. But she was even angrier at the way the two girls were acting – like wet cats. One day she called each one to her separately and told them off. 'You're both utterly simple-minded! You don't have the faintest idea of how to handle men. Whatever they tell you you accept. Did I have you educated just so you could turn into such meek little lambs? You're not inferior to your husbands in any respect. You're equal in education, in family, and furthermore they owe their green cards to you, so stand up to them and assert yourselves!'

Twenty

Tanima's residency was to begin on the first of July. As soon as she started work she found an apartment close to the hospital and moved in with Anuj right away. After this she was constantly reminding Juneja to try to do something for Anuj. 'His grades were better than mine,' she would say, 'but he hasn't been able to find anything at all.'

Unable to disappoint her, Juneja said, 'Yes, I'll certainly dig up something for him.'

Six months later Anuj found a post to replace somebody on leave.

Rakesh was still unemployed. Guddo's burden had been lightened but now envy had been added to Rakesh's frustration. Two residencies in this one family and he was left out in the cold! He said to Anima, 'Why doesn't your mother get Juneja to do something for me?'

'She's spoken to him but if there isn't any vacancy what can she do?'

'Well, couldn't he have given me the position he gave Anuj?'

'But Tanima kept after him. Because she was working in the same hospital she could talk with him every day.'

'Then Tanima should have insisted on getting something for me first. But as I told you, everybody in your family's incredibly selfish. You'd do anything in the world for them. You hand over all your scholarship cheques for house money – but tell me, what do Tanima and Anuj give?'

'But they're not living here now. Why should they contribute anything?'

'Oh great, they're making fifty thousand and we stay here rotting in hell.'

'If you'd found a job first would you have given half your pay to them?'

Rakesh was silent. She went on, 'It was a family matter, whether you got that job or Anuj. And then, who knows whether or not you would have been chosen for it anyway?'

'What do you mean? Are you saying Anuj is smarter than I am?'

'Who's talking about being smart? Everybody's smart here, but what matters is knowing how to take advantage of the right opportunity.'

Anima persuaded Rakesh to take the FRCP exam, which would increase his chance of finding a residency. Tanima was also taking it to consolidate her hold on her position, while Anuj said he would take it next year.

To pay for the training and examination fees cost two and a half months of Anima's scholarship funding. Rakesh and Tanima were scheduled to sit for the exam on the same day, but in different cities. Tanima said to Anima, 'You can come with me to Minneapolis. It's a completely new place for me, I'm getting anxious about it. Anuj can't get off work, so somehow or other you must come. I'll pay for your plane ticket and all that.'

Tanima had been dependent on her sister from the very beginning, and Anima was accustomed to looking after her. But when she spoke to Rakesh about going to Minneapolis he said, 'If you're going to go anywhere, come to Boston with me – or do you care more about your sister?'

'That's not the point, darling. You're a man, you're used to travelling by yourself. But the poor girl is still a child even if she's becoming a doctor. She's had no experience at all going on long trips by herself.'

In the end, she went with Tanima to Minneapolis. That evening Rakesh telephoned her at her hotel. 'I walked out half-way through my exam. Since all you care about is your family there's no reason for me to stay on here. I'm going back to India.'

Anima took the first plane for Boston. By now the exams were over. She found Rakesh pouting like a child; after a lot of persauding she brought him back to New York with her. This behaviour of his both frightened and depressed her. She had no idea of how to establish harmony between him and her family. She had never suspected he was such a baby about everything.

She was aware that he was the youngest of five children, used to being made much of, and living abroad, especially in an atmosphere of failure like this, he missed his family. More than a year had gone by and there was still no job in sight. Anima now began to have doubts about everything concerning their relationship, wondering if she had made a mistake in getting married at all to this spoiled child.

After Tanima and her husband moved out Anima and Rakesh took over their room. Now that they had more time for one another, more time to be together, she tried in every way to establish a happy relationship with him. She kept her weekends free and usually made plans to go somewhere with him. Once, for example, they finally got to Niagara Falls. Anima was overwhelmed by the beauty and splendour of it but Rakesh did not appear impressed. He was more pleased when they went to Atlantic City and he won a few dollars gambling.

There were certain times at night when Anima felt very warm towards Rakesh. But then he would suddenly make a sarcastic remark that pushed her miles away. At times it seemed to her as though his whole spirit had become a rocky cliff full of brambles. Because of the tension she was unable to get closer to him and found herself arguing with him over every trifle. And every time she would have to drink the poison of his disrespect for her and relapse into silence.

And when she saw Anima's distress Guddo was filled with dread.

Twenty-one

Anuj and Tanima's apartment was brand new, light and bright, the kitchen, cabinets and drawers clean and gleaming. Tanima, arranging jars of spices and lentils on the shelves, felt the thrill of having her own home. As soon as she got her first pay cheque she and Anuj gave a dinner party for Guddo, Raju, Anima and Rakesh at an Indian restaurant. Butter chicken, leg of goat, biryani – how they enjoyed it! Since Guddo was a vegetarian they never had such food when they were living with her. It was Tanima, of course, who paid the check since the party was for her family.

She and Anuj had opened separate bank accounts. One day when he was going to buy a medical text book Tanima asked him to buy a book for her. He said, 'Well, give me the money.'

'What – not even a few dollars for your wife?' Tanima was hurt. Though they were husband and wife they had never been able to establish a single identity.

Their residency required the two of them to work thirty-six hours at a stretch; some nights one would be at the hospital, the other at home. Only with difficulty could they manage to spend one day in the week together when they might relax and catch up on sleep.

It was a new illness every day, a new disease, a new kind of treatment, both of them completely immersed in the constant cycle of learning and practice.

Instead of coming together in harmony the habit of competition was getting ever stronger in them. It had been like that in college too. But at that time, when Tanima's grades were lower than Anuj's, she would be pleased. But naturally she wanted with all her heart for him not to think her inferior to himself in intellect. So between them there was a continuing struggle for each to prove himself – neither would acknowledge defeat.

Three months later they took out a loan and bought a car. Guddo was delighted. Even though it belonged to her daughter and son-in-law, still now there was a car in the family. With its arrival she felt that her own status had been raised a notch. At the same time Raju was admitted to Yale University, so the car had come at a most opportune moment. Next August when he left home for college they would be able to drive him up to New Haven.

Tanima was also learning how to drive. But Anuj objected. 'It's a new car,' he said, 'you don't know how to handle it properly. For the time being I'll be the only one to drive it.'

But Tanima passed her driving test and got her licence. One day when Anuj was at the hospital she suddenly decided to take the car and drive over to Guddo's place. She herself was astonished at her new skill. As she went up the stairs to the apartment she was screaming, 'Look, Mummy, I've driven the car all by myself!'

Then she drove Guddo, Raju, Anima and Rakesh around and brought them home again. But on her way back, when she came out on the highway, she collided with another car. Though she suffered only minor bruises the car was a total wreck.

Anuj was wild with rage and shouted, 'Just watch out if you ever touch any car of mine again!'

'It wasn't my fault at all, the other car just came head-on and hit me.'

'No matter whose fault it was, why the devil did you take the car in the first place?'

'Don't worry, the insurance will pay us enough to buy a new one.'

The two of them went on arguing. If Anuj wouldn't let her drive the new car, Tanima said, 'Who cares, I'll buy a car just for me.'

And this is what happened. After only a month there were now two cars in the family. But between Anuj and Tanima there was still no peace.

One Saturday when they both had a day off the phone rang. Tanima answered, then handed the phone to Anuj. For an hour and a quarter he chatted with a girl named Meenakshi. Afterwards Tanima could not resist asking who she was.

'I met her in the hospital, she's an intern. She's settled over here.'

'But you were talking with her as though she was a close friend.'

'So what? She can be a friend too, can't she?'

'Anuj, we haven't even celebrated our third wedding anniversary yet and you're already getting interested in other women. I don't like this at all.'

'Okay, if you don't like it, I'll see that she won't phone me at home any more.'

'So you'll just get together with her away from home!'

'Well, you can't prevent me, you know.' He said this in a joking way, but Tanima did not take it as a joke. She said:

'Look, Anuj, if you start playing around don't think I'll just sit quiet and do nothing. I'm not dependent on you for anything. Our marriage was based on love, and if there isn't any love then the marriage doesn't mean anything any more.'

'You're getting angry just because I chatted and laughed a little with somebody. I'm not seriously involved with anyone.'

Tanima said nothing.

'You know, I really think now that I shouldn't have got myself married before I came to America. I keep meeting so many smart and free-spirited girls here but I'm trapped, I have to suppress my feelings. Why don't you and I come to a compromise? I won't impose any restrictions on you and you won't impose any on me.'

When she heard this Tanima was utterly stunned. 'How dare you say such a thing! You're just garbage and you want to drag me down into the mud with you!'

Later, Tanima heard rumours from some Indian doctor friends that Anuj was flirting with one or two nurses. Dr Juneja too had hinted about this to Guddo. When Tanima heard it from her mother she was convinced it must be true. That evening all hell broke loose in the apartment. Tanima shouted, 'I don't have to go on living with you. I could never imagine you were so rotten. I'm going to file for divorce tomorrow.'

Anuj attempted to calm her down. 'Why can't you understand? Sex and love are two different things. The love I feel for you I could never feel for anybody else. Up till now I really haven't done anything at all, but if I should that ought not to make any difference in our relationship. Forget all this nonsense about divorce. You're such a child! You believe whatever anybody says.'

'Then you must promise never to do anything like that.'

'I promise. I won't.'

But Tanima could no longer trust him.

Guddo was even more grieved by this development. All her labouring and suffering for her children's well-being was resulting only in harm. These tensions in her daughters' lives had frustrated all her aspirations for them. She wondered if she had gone wrong. Had she just been led on by her own selfish desires? *Om vishvani deva savitarduritani parasuva. Yad bhadram tanna asuva* – Remove our grief far from us oh Lord, giver of joy! May we be granted all beneficial virtues, nature, deeds and material objects . . .

Guddo's voice trembled, her vision blurred. All she could say to Anuj was, 'Tanima's very hurt when you do things like that.'

Anuj interrupted her in a voice so harsh that she was shocked: 'I don't think you should interfere in our personal affairs.'

And this Rakesh, who was still eating them out of house and home, how he snarled at Anima! 'Your mother has the nerve to say that I should take out the rubbish. What the hell does she think I am? And to make things worse, now she's beginning to nag about expenses. As though money were everything – you can't take it with you, you know. Why should I be grateful for every little thing she does for her daughters?'

Guddo had centred her whole widow's existence in the lives of these children and now everything was ripping apart at the seams.

Finally she had to go begging for a job for Rakesh. She pleaded with Dr Juneja to do something for him.

Wiping away her tears, Juneja said, 'Uma, you don't have to ask me. I haven't forgotten about him. In fact, you have so many troubles that I haven't wanted to cause you any more sorrow by telling you about my own. As you know, my nephew is also working in this hospital. Someone's complained that I'm giving too many jobs to Indians and they've started an investigation. Now, as it happens, I have solid proof that the three Indians I've hired were better qualified than all the other applicants. You remember that when Tanima was interning here I said to you how lucky this hospital was to get such a brilliant and hard-working young woman. I feel the same about Anuj and my nephew, and not only I but the other members of the selection committee as well. The decision was unanimous, so this investigation is bound to find in my favour. All the same, I'm obliged to proceed with caution. Now: it happens that a vacancy's come up in a hospital in a small town in New Jersey, about twenty miles from here. I'll see about getting the post for Rakesh.'

It took another four months to settle the position. Rakesh was to join the hospital in New Jersey starting in July. Guddo and Anima were both even happier than Rakesh about his getting a job. He had also found an apartment there. Anima was sure that all the complaining and peevishness brought on by his frustration would now cease, and she enjoyed imagining the pleasure of their living in their own apartment.

She and Rakesh moved to the new apartment in July. Then, in August, they all drove Raju up to Yale in Tanima's car. It seemed that now at last the whole family was settled. And all of a sudden, Guddo's apartment was empty.

Twenty-two

Anima was trying to get her life started up again on a new footing. Although he was very busy at the hospital, Rakesh was still discontented. He had always wanted to gain special competence in general medicine but his residency was in paediatrics. In this country the children were generally healthier than elsewhere, and as a result a paediatrician tended to earn less money – another reason Rakesh did not want to enter the field. But the choice was not in his hands.

One day when he came home Anima was sitting waiting for him. 'We're off next Saturday,' she said. 'Let's go to the opera, there's a good Italian company performing just now.'

Rakesh's answer took her completely by surprise. 'This Italian opera stuff isn't for me, my dear. If we have to go out, then let's have dinner in some good Indian or Chinese restaurant. Afterwards, if you like we can go to a disco. I've been thinking, when my first cheque comes we should buy a VCR. Then we can watch Indian movies any time we want. I've really been longing to see some Hindi films.'

Anima had started going to the opera and ballet with Najma. She had always been interested in music and dance, and she regretted not having kept up with it. She thought that when Rakesh joined her they would go to performances together. But since he was indifferent, she enjoyed Western theatre in company with Jane and Najma. Few Indians living in America took any interest at all in American art and culture. For them America was a golden goose with whose utility they were very well

117

acquainted indeed but whose beauty was of absolutely no account.

It was probably her association with Najma that inclined Anima, despite her great respect for Indian civilisation, to want to maintain her contact with the local culture. She was also beginning to take a closer look at society and politics as well. She was surprised never to have found any Indian settled here taking an active part in American politics. Last year Indians living in New York had formed an organisation which joined together several local groups. Anima attended one of their functions and listened to the president of the Federation deliver a fiery speech: 'We've been living in this country so many years, yet we have no real knowledge of it. So we must all be united, so that when the occasion arises we may emerge as a solid Indian minority. Our children will be adults here tomorrow . . . we must remove the thorns from their path so they may live happily here. Indians are not given top positions because it's said that they have no understanding of the people and conditions of this country. You've surely heard how Dr Mangal's promotion at the Community Hospital was blocked for several years because he's an Indian. But now, with pressure from the Federation, he's finally won his promotion. He's not only the senior member of the hospital staff but his work has earned universal praise as well. By being united there's no limit to what we can achieve.'

Anima recalled that after the meeting the Federation's vice-president said, 'I wasn't seated at the chief table – those bastards gave the seat to Patel. After all the money I've invested in this organisation they go and make up to that idiot. If people like Patel and Mehta get all the credit I'm going to withdraw from the Federation.'

The meeting had hardly ended before the members began breaking up into different factions squabbling together, all of them driven by the desire for their own self-advancement.

The Federation had also taken it upon itself to celebrate the Indian holidays. On the fifteenth of August, the parade, in which Indians from all over the country marched, was the main attraction. Other organisations were having Hindu temples built

118

in various parts of the United States. Indian newspapers were coming out with Indian news for Indians, Indian radio and television programmes were starting up in all the big cities.

All these temples and tiny groups, Anima thought, had only one aim: we don't want to be lost, we don't want to sink in this immense ocean. We've pitched our tents on the shore; we want to enjoy the warmth and light of its sun but we're afraid of being overwhelmed by its waves. Here too the *gurdvaras* provided anchors, but how many Indians were willing to offer money to set up soup-kitchens for the poor and homeless?

Each Indian here was a merchant in the great market of America. He came with his brains, knowledge and experience, ready to auction himself off. If he brought a good price, all the better: a fine job, a beautiful home, an attractive wife, a blonde girlfriend – this was the best deal you could get. And even though they didn't fetch so high a price, there were always jobs as waiters or doormen anyway, which all in all didn't seem such a bad deal either.

But of course there was a loss of integrity when a less educated, less able American girl like Janet became Guddo's supervisor, or when Raju's character was moulded as he sat, silent and inert, glued to the TV, or when you had to support husbands bought at the price of a green card or, if you didn't support them, the destiny of so many girls was marred by the bitterness of divorce. A loss that could not be made up by a feverish building of new marble temples, *gurdvaras*, and Vedic universities.

And these temple organisations, Anima thought, are only meant to satisfy the Indians' psychological and social hungers. Everything goes on in the temples. People don't really go there for worship.

Anyway, as soon as you get here India becomes totally irrelevant. All the same, we keep our ear tuned for news from over there. So we actually aren't committed anywhere at all. We easily shake off any concern for either country. On the whole, life keeps circling around earning money and acquiring various kinds of material things to enjoy.

And that certainly is just what Guddo, her daughters and their husbands were doing, as Anima realised. For her part, Tanima was aware of that materialism in a different way: she maintained that Anuj needed not things but live female bodies for enjoyment. Suspicion had bitten deep into her. Interrogations and quarrels every moment.

'You weren't at the hospital yesterday. Where did you go?'

'Yesterday? Oh yes, yesterday I went to a bar with some friends.'

'What friends?'

'You know, Amar and Ajay.'

'Why didn't you take me? I was at home doing nothing.'

'What do I know about your plans? You should stick your schedule on the door of the fridge. Anyway, can't I spend a little time with my friends once in a while? And you don't like going to bars. You once said it was better for people to stay home rather than be bored in some bar.'

'That's true, but that didn't mean I was supposed to stay home while you wasted money in bars. We have so little time with one another as it is, and what's more . . .'

Tanima suspected Anuj was spending his money on women and liquor, and so she was keeping the money she'd earned strictly under her own control. Guddo had also urged her to be extremely prudent, for who could tell when a man like that might get seriously involved with some other woman. So Tanima's love for Anuj, which formerly had been so spontaneous and passionate, was beginning to fade.

One day the fridge was empty. Neither Tanima nor Anuj had done any grocery shopping. When he came back from the hospital Anuj was ravenous; when he found nothing in the fridge he went into a rage.

'This is your day off, so if you're not going to cook you might at least have shopped for something.'

Tanima was sitting on the sofa, reading. 'Yesterday,' she said, 'was your day off, wasn't it? You could have done the shopping. Anyway, I didn't have any ready cash.'

'Meaning?'

'Meaning I would have had to go to the bank to get some and

I didn't have that much time.' Then she could no longer hold back the words churning inside her. 'I've never said anything about it but your carelessness is getting worse and worse. You know the man is responsible for taking care of the household expenses. If I just keep quiet about it you go on expecting more and more. But this is your duty, not the wife's. While I spend my whole salary looking after the house you're out having fun or wasting your money on expensive presents for your mother and father. When I said we might help Raju with his education by giving a little money you said, "Your brother isn't our responsibility." And you're an old-fashioned conservative too. Of course they used to have the custom of the dowry when women were entirely dependent on men, but now that we're both equal why don't you stand up and oppose those old ways? It's only where girls are concerned that you've opened up – when it comes to them you're a great defender of free relations! If you want freedom for yourself you'd better learn to give it to others too!'

For once, Anuj had nothing to say.

Twenty-three

Pregnant now, Tanima felt pierced by so many thorns that she thought she must be bleeding. She had made a marriage of her choice, so why this suffering? Obsessed with advancing in their careers, she and Anuj had drawn further and further apart and found no time left for one another. Tanima said to Guddo:

'Mummy, if the foundation's cracked is there any point in pouring cement over it? I don't want to have this baby.'

'You're grown up, my dear, you're intelligent. Make whatever decision you want and act on it. The only thing that will make me happy is seeing you happy.'

'The truth is, right now my career is the most important thing. If I drop out in the middle of my residency, what will I do later on? I've spent so many years getting educated to be a doctor, and all my hard work could just go down the drain.'

'Won't it hurt you terribly to do it?' Guddo said a bit timidly.

Tears started up Tanima's eyes. 'Mummy, I really can't figure out what my relationship with this man is. He says he loves me, and then . . . but I can't think any more about that now. There isn't much time left.'

When Anuj learned about the abortion he went into a rage. He slapped Tanima on the cheek and said, close to screaming, 'How could you do it! I wrote just yesterday to my family with the good news. What are they going to say? How could you be so inhuman?'

Tanima felt weak in both body and spirit. She kept having the horrible feeling that she had lost something forever, something that would not come back no matter how much she might want it. Always that feeling of having lost a treasure. Sitting beside her, Guddo kept her head close to the pillow. 'Is there any pain, darling?'

'No pain . . .' Tanima sounded as though drifting off, lost. 'I feel . . . I keep having such strange thoughts . . . Anuj is laying his head in my lap . . . his face looks awfully loving . . . then suddenly it's distorted . . . I say to him . . . but I don't know what I say to him . . . but Mummy, why did he hit me like that? I probably did the right thing . . . if he couldn't belong to me even though he was my husband how could he have my child, my motherhood? Anuj seems so sad to me. But now I can't give it back to him. I can only make a promise for the future.'

But who has ever seen the future? Tanima became pregnant two more times. She caught chicken-pox the first time and the baby had to be aborted. The second time the child's brain was undeveloped; after the tests the doctors advised that it would be much better for such a child to die rather than be brought into the world. So Tanima was cheated of her desire to have a child.

*

Guddo reflects that one has to pay the price for every bit of happiness. She begins to tremble violently from head to foot as she prays:

'Oh Lord, let there be no obstacles to the fulfillment of this sacrifice!'

Twenty-four

When her cousins were married Radhika had said sarcastically that Guddo was making a regular business of importing husbands from India. She had never imagined anyone could arrange marriages in this way. Aunt Guddo struck her as a quaint sort of relative from the old country, while Guddo thought the girl was lacking in respect to her elders and was very offended by it. She even made a point of mentioning it to Gita, who was herself much disturbed by her daughter's attitude. She expressed her concern to Guddo:

'Bringing up girls is the hardest work in this country. If you try to control them, then you think, maybe you're keeping them chained up all for nothing, and if you don't keep a tight rein, they just break out like a cyclone. And if you try to find some middle path, it always turns out to be a mistake. Just look at Radhika and her friends, crowding together out there in the streets in front of the apartment buildings. I worry because who knows when these girlfriends will turn into boys and my daughter will suddenly find herself in a lot of trouble.'

'Have you explained all this to her?' Guddo asked.

'When has she ever let anyone explain anything to her? While you're still talking she'll start screaming that she knows all about everything so why am I jabbering at her.'

'One day,' said Guddo, 'I heard her asking Anima what she and Rakesh used so she wouldn't get pregnant.'

Gita felt something like a current of electricity flash through her. So her fears were not false!

Radhika's complexion was turning sallow. Then nausea and

vomiting. She herself did not know what was happening to her. She thought it was just something ordinary, perhaps a matter of diet, and she said to her mother, 'Everything you cook is so greasy, it makes me nauseous.'

Suspicious, Gita said, 'But even boiled vegetables make you throw up. Tomorrow I'm taking you to the doctor. You seem to be getting weaker all the time.'

The doctor asked Gita, 'Is she married?'

Gita felt her blood run cold. 'No.'

'Well, she'll have to have a pregnancy test.'

Gita came close to fainting. There were blisters on Radhika's body, very big blisters. Messengers of fear, anxiety and shame! When she got home Gita beat her breast and sobbed. 'My fate is cursed! That such things should happen to me! If only we hadn't lost our mines! If only we hadn't come here! Kiran went back to India with her daughters as soon as they were older. Why are we stuck here? What's here for us? And now . . . now there's no way out. She hasn't even left us any way to hide our shame. And Kanika – why doesn't something happen to her to finish us all off? All these girls going to school and college . . . how can you keep your eye on her every minute of the day? Should we tie her up with a rope?' And she went on babbling, 'She told me the other girls have boyfriends so why shouldn't I? "Mummy, why don't you let me do what everybody else does?" Now you see what's happened. How could she be so stupid?'

Jijaji striking her again and again, one blow after another. Say whatever has to be said: Radhika had been incited by some demonic power. Only when Jijaji began to howl and roar did Gita come to her senses. Taking pity on Radhika, she said, 'She's lying there half-dead already so why beat her? If you want to kill her that's something else, just strangle her, it will be easy. At least there's no shame in dying.'

The phone rang: Pinki inviting them all to Arjun's birthday party on Sunday.

And Gita, her voice faint: 'Can't say . . . we may not be able to come. Radhika's quite ill.'

'We've got three doctors in the family!' Pinki's voice at the other end of the line. 'They'll know what to do for her.' And Gita's cautious answer:

'No, no, Jijaji's terribly busy. Working overtime. Please don't insist.'

An atmosphere of mourning had settled on Gita's home. Her husband didn't eat for three days. The investment and work of a whole lifetime laid waste in one trick of fate – for what misdeeds was this the reward? Failure, pain and rage breathing poisonous flames. Sometimes absolute silence and sometimes running to Gita, roaring:

'I always told you, use a little discipline with her. Even now you're spoiling her, cooking special things. I tell you, throw her out of the house. She can't stay here disgracing me.'

'What are you saying? If she can't stay here would you have her out on the street? Will your disgrace stay out there with her? Whatever else, she's still a child. Do you think she can be grown up at sixteen? She'll be getting an abortion, so what are you worrying about? She'll be back to normal in four days.'

But would she really be normal? Could this stain ever be washed away? So many many wounds! She doubted all of them could ever be healed.

Radhika's fear of surgical instruments was so great that at the mere thought of them she would begin to shake. What if I should die? she wondered, remembering that sometimes there could be fatal infections. Could her life end so soon? She wanted to do a lot more living. She would lay her head in her mother's lap and sob, 'Save me, Mummy, please! Save me . . .'

Gita was frightened. They shouldn't be shouting abuse at her, she was already suffering enough. Gita would stroke her head, draw her fingers through the girl's long thick hair, and say, 'Everything's going to be all right, darling. In future be more careful.' Then they would hear her husband thundering:

'You're wasting a lot of sympathy on this little bitch, aren't you? Cradling her in your lap like that! If you so much as touch her your hands will get filthy.' The very moment he saw Radhika he felt as though a forest of sharp thorns were springing up all over his body.

126

Radhika was to begin college next year. She had said, 'I'll share a room with somebody when I go. It scares me just to look at Papa. Anyway, studying at home won't work out, so much time would be wasted going back and forth to school.'

Kanika, by now studying medicine at some distance from New York, was already living in a college dorm. So Gita was distressed at the thought that her home would soon be deserted. Ashok too spent most of his time away from the apartment. But she had to put Radhika on her feet. Here there was as much pressure for getting girls to amount to something on their own, away from home, as there was for boys. And then, the way the girl turned out would decide the kind of husband she'd get. More important even than the family was the value put on the girl herself. A woman here could be made whole only by enduring these pressures.

Gita looked at herself, at Guddo, at Anima. She was forced to work, since the burden of supporting the whole family was on her shoulders. Guddo might manage both her home and her job all by herself, but Anima was of the next generation. But though she was a woman of the next generation and wanted to live like one, her husband was in opposition and would not let her get ahead. Guddo had heard Rakesh say, 'We're not like those men who turn into their wives' slaves. Cooking meals is not for us. It's okay to drive a car and take our wives around in them, but all this business of cooking and cleaning is not our work.'

And this generation of Radhika's! Were they all really so irresponsible? How many of them became mothers while still in high school, how many girls dropped out early to look after their kids! Playing with dolls came quickly to an end for them. Reality was outside. These boys and girls, without learning how to swim, diving into the ocean and drowning in the roaring waves of the first assault of economic pressures. The man would flounder and struggle to keep above water. And the child-mother, with her curse in her lap, left in midstream, suffering the blows of fortune, being hustled off to the psychiatric wards or knocking at the doors of a social welfare office.

But Gita was going to save her daughter. Really save her.

Radhika *would* go to college. She'd stand on her own two feet, even though, long before, she'd said so stubbornly, 'What's the point of going to college? I don't want to keep on studying. There's a lot more to life! I want to find out all about living, not turn into a bookworm.' And then, 'Just give me a grace period of two years. During that time I'll find out all about myself, after that I'll go to college.'

This frightened Gita. 'If you pass up college just once it will be forever. You're going to go to college. This is something we absolutely insist on.'

Radhika applied to a college that was considered rather mediocre and was admitted.

Twenty-five

Arun, the taxi driver, and his American wife, Judy, had become regular visitors to Guddo's apartment. Judy had been coming to Guddo to learn Hindi and a strong affection had grown up between them.

Guddo wondered occasionally how it was that although Judy was a woman of this time and place she in no way supported the women's movement. To look at her you'd think she was a quite ordinary, if rather sensitive, girl. But how had Arun produced such a tempest in her life? He had her dangling in mid-air on a thread of indecision while he himself kept dangling. Yesterday something very odd had happened – even now Guddo could hardly believe it.

Arun had come to the apartment with mangoes, papadum and sweets. He said to Guddo:

'Didi, it looks as though my mother and father are all set to get me married.'

Bewildered, Guddo asked, 'But how can that be?'

'They're having a look at some girls over there. One girl really pleased them a lot. They said she'd adapt very easily to the ways of our house. And – I said yes. The engagement will be formalised in a week.'

Guddo was shocked. 'What? You mean you've just gone and agreed to this?'

'What could I do? It's all been arranged by my mother and father, and the way they're counting on it I was afraid that if I refused one of them would surely have a heart attack – especially my mother. She already has heart trouble.'

129

'But you're already married . . . and what's going to happen to Judy?'

'I haven't told her yet.'

Angry now, Guddo said, 'How can you deceive somebody you live with like this?'

'It's not a question of deception but necessity. Didi, if you were in my place you'd understand. My mother's been dreaming all her life of bringing my bride into the house with all the fanfare and ceremony, a real beauty all wrapped in her sari – how can I disappoint her? My relationship with my mother is the most important one in my life.'

'And you didn't even think of Judy!'

'Well, you know, things aren't going too well with us these days. As for this girl, the red tape will take a whole year. So for at least a year there's no need to tell Judy. I'll break away gradually.'

'Don't you realise you have a responsibility to Judy too? You know how emotional she is, and when she hears about your marriage . . .'

'I've already told her over and over again that my parents would never consent to my marrying her.'

'That doesn't mean you have to bow to their wishes and hurt Judy this way. Anyway, you *are* married to her.'

'Of course I know that, Didi, but you don't understand what it means to be an only son.'

'What I'm thinking is, you ought to have some guts and tell her straight out. The way you're acting now you're not only messing up your own life but other people's lives too.'

On Sundays Judy often drove to Guddo's in her car and took her and Raju out for a ride. But Arun hardly ever joined them. They would ride up to Bear Mountain to see the hills or the zoo, or for a picnic on the banks of the Hudson. On the way home Raju would watch the stars and say, 'Look at the sky, how bright the moon and stars are!' For it was true that moon and stars were nowhere to be seen when you were surrounded by the tall buildings of the city. At such moments Guddo would invoke her gods . . . Sun, Moon . . . *Om Suryo Jyotih Jyotih Suryah Svaha* . . .

but where was the light? For her heart was covered with darkness, her sky had shrunk to nothing.

'I can't sleep nights,' Judy said to Guddo sadly. 'I guess I don't understand Indian men. Does Arun really love me? I don't know why I keep feeling so afraid. I feel as though there's something in his life I don't have any part in.'

And Guddo thought that there was something in Raju's life too that she herself had no part in.

While Radhika – inside her there was an agitation which neither Gita nor anyone else could share. As for what was happening inside Arjun – that was something Pinki could not suspect.

Twenty-six

During the summer vacation Raju came home, loaded with books and work.

'You shouldn't stay buried in your books all through the vacation,' Guddo told him. 'Go out and have some fun.'

'Where could I go? These same old streets, the same old things!'

'We'll make plans to go and see new places. Shall I speak to Tanima?'

'No, there's no time. Going out driving would waste too much time. I have lots of work to get through.'

'What kind of work are you doing?'

'You wouldn't understand, Mother. I have to solve all kinds of problems involving math and computers. I've got to do something really important, invent something I can get patented, and then I'll be a millionaire.'

Guddo thought he was aiming for the stars. He was so capable, her son, so ambitious, and surely he would accomplish something significant . . .

*

'*Kamanam samarddhavitre sarvannah svaha*,' Guddo chants above the sacrificial fire. 'Oh Lord who in the form of Agni fulfills all desires, I make this offering to you.'

As she throws the sacrificial objects into the fire a tiny spark touches Guddo's fingers.

*

How many units of time had come and gone! Days, months, years. Guddo asked Arun, 'Have you sent for your bride yet?'

Arun looked at her anxiously. 'I can't understand it, Didi. I don't know what's happened to me. I scold Judy for nothing at all. And I'm angry with my parents too. They keep writing, asking when I'm going to send for the girl, her family's getting very worried. They write that people are talking, saying I've married someone else over here. The girl's father is practically grovelling before my father, saying he's being dishonoured. But what can I do?'

After reflecting, Guddo finally said, 'I want to tell you, but there's no point in it. You should have thought about all this first. The question now is, what are you going to decide?'

'I'm thinking, for life over here a wife from here is the right thing. And the one over there, well, I don't know her character, her ideas, how she'd manage . . . I don't know anything at all about her.'

'So?'

'I'm writing to my parents to arrange an annulment somehow or other.'

'What!'

'Yes, the betrothal ceremony's already been performed, so there's nothing else to be done.'

'Do you think this won't break your parents' hearts now? And what will happen to that girl whose life you've just ruined? Who can tell if she'll be able to arrange a second marriage or not. How do you know she's not the sensitive sort of girl who'll take poison?'

She was angry with him because he couldn't make a decision. A tremendous inner struggle was going on inside him that not only tormented him but was eating up all the people around him too. He was never going to be free of his mother, or of Judy either.

A story in the newspaper told of how an Indian engineer had committed suicide by pouring gasoline over himself and setting himself on fire on his lawn. He appeared in the photo with his wife and three children. When she read it Guddo was terribly upset. The man had a good job, all the things to bring him prosperity and happiness, and still he chose to die. Why? Was it

133

the same canker of loneliess that was eating Guddo up inside? That suicide, despite having a whole family of his own, had felt himself utterly alone. And now Guddo's house was empty, all the young birds had flown off to their own nests. Would Raju stay with her in her old age? In this blind and stupefying race for material gain who could stop for anybody else? Everybody's destiny was somehow suspended between two worlds. The heart there, the body here, the mother there, the lover here ... the sense of the glorious past in one place, in the other the hunger for a present without savour.

Even if Arun's mother came over what solution could they find? Then the mother's destiny would also be split between here and there. Only think of Pinki's mother-in-law, who'd come over because both her sons were in America. One day she told Guddo how miserable she was:

'Can you call this a life here? No one to visit, no one to talk to! What can you do all alone and lonesome? And how can you cook properly or eat the right things? People eat sandwiches. They just cook one real meal, that's all. And my Arjun ... what do you call them, pizzas, yes, he eats pizzas or those round, round things, what are they, hamburgers, yes, he just fills up on hamburgers. I can't understand what they've got here that makes everybody want to come.'

Satinder's mother found her whole life here completely restricted. No neighbours to come and visit and have tea with, no acquaintances, no cook or washerman or sweeper to share in her life, nor even any relatives close by or distant who would come and stay for days without having to be invited and whose visits were always a source of pleasure or complaint. Nor were there any of the familiar streets or familiar people available so that when you were bored at home you could step out on those streets. No street at all led to a friend or relative's home where you drank your tea, praised or slandered someone, and the day went by. The world of the home was not really separate from the life outside it as it was in New York. One felt at home outside as well ... the familiar grocer's shop, the rickshaw man everybody knew, the well-known film songs blasting forth from the *paan* shop on the corner. But here outside the apartment there was such an overwhelming flood of strangeness that she was frightened and wouldn't venture out. She'd say over and over again, 'Let me go back. But even there what peace can I find now? Writing letters back and forth . . . if my sons are here how can I be happy in my lonely house?' The destiny of the sons had suspended their mother between two worlds.

Satinder, Pinki's husband, agreed that bringing his mother over was a mistake. She was completely cut off from everything around her.

But who wasn't? Guddo, Gita, Anima, Tanima, Raju. Still, it was even harder for Satinder's mother – she spoke no English at all so she couldn't communicate with anybody outside the family.

But even when they spoke English, could you say that Guddo or Raju or Jijaji knew how to communicate?

Kanika had obtained a residency in surgery. Though she was twenty-four now, Gita was upset when a graduation party was planned for her: surely they shouldn't send Kanika to a dinner and dance party all by herself. So Kanika shouldn't mind if Pinki, her youngest aunt, went along with her. As the saying goes, once you've burned your tongue on hot milk you're extra cautious even when they tell you it's cold. Even at twenty-four a daughter needs watching.

Pinki did go but she thought it was ridiculous. Kanika spent her time chatting confidentially with her fellow medical students. Michel, a tall and elegant young black man, led her onto the dance floor. They both looked happy dancing together. In her white dress, with its tight belt, Kanika's waist seemed even slimmer. Her partner's hand from time to time would tighten around her waist and draw her closer, and Kanika's body, trembling with embarrassment, would gradually pull away. The other young people were all completely absorbed in one another. Body on body, lip on lip. But now Kanika too was an adult. How long would she continue to be her daddy's clever little pet? Pinki thought it ridiculous to have to keep watch on her like this.

Twenty-seven

One day Gita said to Guddo, 'If we can just find some nice young doctor, then we ought to get Kanika married right away.'

But Kanika was not willing to be married now. She said, 'It's been hard enough just getting through my studies. I want to have a little while to relax and just work the way I feel like working. And then I'll be able to help Radhika and Ashok with their studies too. Anyway, my residency will be beginning in six weeks – and then I'll be rich.'

She knew that when she married she would belong to somebody else. Right now she belonged to herself. And right now she could still help Radhika and Ashok – something that would be against the old-fashioned Indian protocol and an embarrassment to her parents once she had a husband.

And Michel! For his sake too she wanted to delay things. She wondered when she would have the courage to talk to Papa about him. But how could she tell her father? How shocked he'd be! This was a great burden on Kanika's mind. She had always been Papa's good little daughter. And now they were planning to marry her to some nice boy whenever the opportunity arose. So she was afraid to let them know that she had a friend whom she liked so much, and what's more, he was black.

Oh, what a hypocrite you had to be! Why couldn't she just say, 'Papa, I like Michel very much – whether he's black or whatever, he's a doctor and my friend'? But Kanika was afraid lest her father have a heart attack. He already looked so changed, so broken. Silent, sad . . . as though some burden was constantly weighing him down. One day, when he took her back after the

136

weekend, in her apartment at the hospital, he embraced her and said, 'Daughter, you're all I have.' When she looked up at him she saw tears in his eyes.

When she mentioned this to Michel he said, 'Huh . . . emotional blackmail! When children begin to stand on their own feet their parents try to keep controlling them by doing things like that.'

Kanika did not like hearing him say this. From the beginning how her father had loved her, how he devoted all his attention to her! Now it had become 'emotional blackmail'. In her childhood she had been very afraid of her father. As she grew older the fear disappeared. Now she felt sorry for him. It was as though all the vitality had been squeezed out of him. How weak, how small he felt inside himself. One day he said, 'My life has reached as far as it can go. I did nothing . . . I'll die having been nothing but a doorman. Still, you're all here, whatever else happens. I ought to go back to India, there I'll be able to die in peace.'

'Papa,' Kanika broke in, 'what foolish things you're saying, you still have lots of living ahead of you' – that was all she could manage to say.

Thunderous, ear-splitting music. On the small dance floor hundreds of bodies swaying, pressing against one another, pulling away. Glittering lights flashing on and off at their own rhythm, playing with those bodies. Suspended from the middle of the ceiling a big cinema screen on which from time to time there flashed images of naked female figures. The screen would roll down, then rise back up again. Girls, half-naked in the gowns that sheathed them, curly-headed young men heavily made-up, their clothes in disarray. Hair sometimes shaped like peacock fans, sometimes half the head shaved, sometimes shaved on both sides with hair in the middle rising like an open Japanese fan. Crowds of girls of sixteen, every limb gyrating and vibrating with the music. Anima, remaining a mere spectator, stared at these outlandish creatures. This was one of the city's most famous discos. Rakesh had talked about it a lot so she'd come with him

137

to see it. But she didn't feel like dancing, she felt she couldn't be part of this mob. In her *kurta-pajama* she felt like someone who's put on a heavy winter coat in the hot summer weather. She was sweating, she felt as though she were suffocating. Everything happening in the disco seemed completely alien to her, part of somebody else's life – a confused, silly, crazy atmosphere. While from the edge of the dance floor she took in the spectacle of these swaying, intoxicated young men and women she suddenly saw a familiar face, though it was difficult to recognise it under the disco's lights flashing on and off. Suddenly, in one brief illumination she caught a glimpse of Radhika. But a different Radhika: new hair style – the long straight tresses were now waved in a permanent; and even from this distance you could see the glitter of enormous vulgar earrings which reached to her shoulders. And her dress revealed most of the upper part of her body, which struck Anima as terribly thin and fragile. Anima could not restrain herself and plunged onto the dance floor, forcing a way through the crowd until she reached Radhika.

'What are you doing here?' she was close to shouting into her cousin's ear, and as she did she was aware of a strong, unfamiliar smell.

'Having a good time – what are *you* doing here?' said Radhika, and the smell assaulted Anima's nostrils so that she drew back a little.

'Where are you staying nowadays?' she asked.

'I've quit college,' said Radhika. 'I've got a job as a waitress in a nightclub. It's good pay.'

In the deafening noise of the screaming music it was impossible to hold any further conversation. Anima turned and regained her place at the edge of the dance floor. From there she continued to watch Radhika as a rather tall young white American took her in his arms and kissed her.

Rakesh came up to Anima from behind, took her hand, and said, 'Come on, let's go out and dance. What a specatator you've turned into, watching everybody like that! It's really not the way to act in a place like this.'

Rakesh, pushing on her shoulder, moved her out on the dance

floor. There, her thoughts troubled, she went through the motions of the dance automatically, without taking any pleasure in it. It appeared that Radhika was completely at home with these people. Why couldn't I be like that? she wondered. But in fact, she was simply repelled by this whole disco culture and its vulgar noise, which she had already heard in India. To her the people who frequented the disco halls were shallow and stupid. But she couldn't figure out where her own roots were. Every day Rakesh made the point that she had been here for five whole years now and so she ought to apply for American citizenship. She'd finished her PhD and now she had to start looking for a job. But finding one was not going to be easy. Rakesh said that by becoming a citizen the door to many other kinds of jobs would be open to her, jobs which people who were only residents couldn't get. Anima was shocked and confused. She was aware that there was discrimination against Indians in the job market, but she had not expected it to apply to her. She was interested in American art and culture but that didn't mean she wanted to become American. Was her Indian identity to be compromised for the sake of a job?

Anima could not jettison her values all at once. But afraid to lose Rakesh, she went on suppressing her own feelings, doing everything the way he wanted in order to become like an ordinary weak Indian wife. In truth, she had never been able to love Rakesh with all her heart because of his arrogance, his irrepressible male ego and self-concern. If he was at home then Anima was obliged to stay at home to look after him. So she must always return from the university at a particular time, no matter how much work she left unfinished there. Rakesh demanded complete devotion, and Anima neglected everything else to do one thing or another for him, wait for him, schedule everything she did according to his wishes. So long as she complied in every detail he treated her with affection, but the moment she did anything on her own he would either sulk or get angry and shout reproaches at her.

To make matters worse, he had absolutely no use for any of Anima's friends or family. If she ever tried to make plans to visit Tanima or her mother he would make a scene.

'All week long there you are at the university hanging around with God knows who, now even on your day off you don't feel like spending a little time with me.'

'There's no need to get angry. If you don't want to, we won't go. But you know we haven't seen my mother for three months now.'

'So you haven't gone to see her for three months, but what about me? I haven't seen my mother for years while you've got your whole family here. You never think about me, stuck over here in a foreign country with a wife who only cares about other people.'

'I can't figure out what you expect from me. If you want me to stay at home massaging your feet and cooking for you, well, that kind of life isn't for me. Marriage means partnership. The two of us ought to share everything together. But if all you want is to stretch out on the sofa with the newspaper while I slave away in the kitchen, forget it!'

'I've never seen my mother anywhere but in the kitchen, and my father in the easy chair reading the newspaper. And it's going to be just like that here. If you think you can use a lot of big words to soften me up and make me your darling pet you're dead wrong. You're stuck up about your studying and degrees but that doesn't impress me at all. Do whatever you want away from home but here it's up to you to take care of everything. After all, you ought to be grateful – at least I don't forbid you to leave the house.'

Controlling her anger with difficulty, Anima managed to say only, 'It's no disgrace for a man to help out with the housework.'

'Oh yes, that's just what girls like you want – a domesticated husband! The man at home cooking and the woman away enjoying herself.'

'When you decided to marry me what did you expect – a little simpering bride with her veil drawn over her face coming to slave for you? You knew all about my plans for the future.'

Rakesh was astonished. 'You may have been planning on studying and working but didn't I count for anything? You didn't tell me we ought to have a cook or a sweeper – you should have brought him with you.'

Anima flared up. 'You should be ashamed to talk to your wife like that. The truth is, when you married me you were seeing visions of America, you didn't see me at all, you were just dreaming of a lucrative career for yourself. It wouldn't have mattered who was in my place, you were ready to marry anybody you could use. But marriage isn't just a means to get ahead, it's an end in itself. You can't change me, I can't change you so we have to maintain some kind of flexibility with one another. If you insist on remaining a macho man like your old fogy conservative forefathers, well then . . .'

As soon as he heard that word 'macho' the fire flamed up inside Rakesh. 'How dare you!' he shouted. 'I absolutely loathe this women's lib talk of yours. Macho, macho! You call my whole family old fogy conservatives. You and your mother are just old-fashioned whores!'

As his rage mounted he delivered six or seven slaps in quick succession to Anima's cheek.

'Are you a man or an animal?' Anima shouted back. But stupefied by the shock and pain her anger gave way to weeping. The voice of her scorched womanhood told her, 'I can't stay any longer with a man like this. After such disgrace, such dishonour . . . as far as he's concerned I'm nothing.'

That whole night Anima, lying on one side of the double bed, kept tossing and turning while Rakesh lay on the other side. Neither made any effort to appease the other. The fire of their anger burned still deeper, and there was no sign of any cooling shower anywhere. A profound regret was boiling inside Anima. She should never have married! Why couldn't she have opposed her mother? She ought never to have agreed. She'd got nothing out of this marriage except anger, aggravation, worry and now slaps. Between Rakesh's outlook and her own there was an unbridgeable gulf. Either she would have to give up everything she wanted and go on being a domestic, obedient kind of little wife to fit into Rakesh's mother's mould, or else find freedom by breaking off this relationship completely the way one cuts a diseased limb from the body.

On the surface how good everything seemed! Just as, while an ulcer spreads poison inside, for a long time the body outwardly appears perfectly normal. There was the affectionate mother, a tranquil, impressive father, Rakesh's stature, his commanding personality; an educated doctor, courteous and well-mannered – everything one expects to see in a future husband. But she was unable to see whatever else there was, she'd been given no opportunity to discover it. If she had, she wouldn't have had to put up with this suffering, this hell. Now she meant nothing to anybody.

Lying on the other side of the bed, Rakesh kept attacking over and over again the image he had of Anima as a stubborn, conceited girl. If this is what comes of educating a woman, then you could throw education out the window. How hurt his mother would be if she knew what kind of daughter-in-law had come into the family. He would invite her over, she might be able to teach this silly girl something. How dare she call him an old-fashioned conservative! The more liberty he gave her the more outrageous she became. Though maybe he himself should try a little tenderness . . . it wasn't right to strike her . . . maybe a little loving would bring her round. She was his wife, after all . . .

As soon as the word 'wife' came into his mind a tender emotion woke in Rakesh. He moved just a little closer to Anima and began to stroke her body. But Anima was drained emotionally: there was no reaction, neither acceptance nor rejection, to his probing fingers.

142

Twenty-eight

When Guddo came home from the office, feeling tired and defeated, the telephone was ringing. It was Anima, weeping while she recounted last night's incident. 'What am I going to do, Mummy? I can't go on like this.'

Guddo was alarmed. Things were getting much worse, but it wouldn't be right to upset Anima even more. After all, everybody had to make adjustments in a marriage.

'Darling, these are just "teething troubles"', she told her. 'Fights like this go on in every marriage, and then everything works out. It wouldn't be right to think of separating over such a trifle.'

'It's not a trifle,' said Anima, angry. 'You just don't understand.' And she hung up.

It was one of those days when things got worse and worse. Anima had hardly hung up when the phone rang again. It was Pinki, calling to tell Guddo that Gita's husband had had a stroke.

This was almost too much, Guddo thought. The tensions over the children had been going on more or less constantly, but nothing as serious as this had ever happened over here before. True, Guddo had never had much use for her brother-in-law, but she suffered for her sister and Gita's children. But then she also could not help reminding herself that Jijaji was no longer of much use. If he died it would not be as painful for Gita as the death of Guddo's husband had been for her. For Gita this death would bring about no particular change in the way she led her life. And the children were all grown up by now. Kanika was already earning considerably more than her father. But as for what someone might feel at the emotional level, Guddo did not try to imagine.

Pinki was saying, 'Kanika's had him admitted to the hospital. As soon as Satinder comes we'll all drive over to see him.'

'But it's awfully late already ... Couldn't we go in the morning. Oh – but tomorrow morning I have to go to the bank. Why don't we go tomorrow evening?'

'Gita just phoned to tell me he's still unconscious.'

'Then for the moment,' Guddo said, 'there's no point in going to see him.'

So, feeling only a little guilty, she thought that maybe it would be time enough if she finally got to see him at the weekend.

When Jijaji regained consciousness his memory was completely gone and he was unable to recognise anyone. Life, which had dealt him so many heavy blows in the past, was gradually fading for him. How could he want to remember such a bitter present?

Gita could not hold back her tears. Jijaji was going to have to stay in the hospital indefinitely. Her heart and soul, mind and body, were stretched out on a hospital bed. Kanika was constantly on the run, checking various tests, talking with doctors, her face masked to appear as though everything was perfectly natural while she listened to the deliberations about Papa's fate and took on the painful duty of bringing the news to her mother.

'We have to live with it,' she told Gita. 'Half of Papa's body is paralysed.'

'But he *will* recover won't he?'

Kanika sometimes acted like a daughter, sometimes like a doctor. She would say such things as: 'Well, with this kind of stroke the victim doesn't recover. But Papa still might get over it. Just bear up and don't be discouraged. Papa could live a very long time in this condition and if his condition worsens . . .' But the word 'death' never passed her lips.

The standard for all her accomplishments had been her father. Now they meant nothing to him. He had forgotten Kanika . . .

When a living person lost his memory how terrible it was for those close to him.

When Guddo saw Jijaji lying there, helpless, half-dead, she wept for him too. How powerless humans were!

In Gita's home silent death was lurking, and inside her it was as though a saw were slicing her up. What was she going to do, alone in a foreign country? Was he never going to come home again? Kanika said, 'Mummy, try to forget Papa. It's most unlikely that he'll recover. With a stroke like this only one out of a hundred gets better.'

And Gita felt like Savitri yearning to bring Satyavan back from the dead.

For her part, Guddo was now truly beginning to accept the dictates of fate . . . you die when it's destined. All those years before, the medicines hadn't yet reached India for her own husband. While here they had all the medicines, and Jijaji, because his daughter had become a doctor, was getting even better care . . . and still . . .

Radhika came home to ask about her father, and this brought an outburst from Kanika. 'You're responsible for all this,' she said. 'If it weren't for the wicked way you've acted Papa wouldn't be in this state today. You bitch, get out of this house!'

Gita was crushed. What Kanika said was true, and she could only curse her own bad luck. Among hundreds of thousands they could have a daughter like Kanika who cared so much for her mother and father, and then give birth to a dreadful little misfit like Radhika. Stubborn, wilful, no sense at all of right and wrong. This was luck indeed!

Everybody's despair and suffering acted like stings to bite deep into Radhika. It hurt most to think that nobody was aware of what *she* was suffering.

When she went back home Radhika felt sick at heart.

She had not committed any crime, she considered herself completely innocent. But right up to this very day her parents and Kanika had always accused her of some fault or other. Now they were making her responsible for Papa's condition. Could that really be true? Radhika felt like screaming and sobbing, she'd done nothing wrong, they mustn't accuse her.

Her conviction that she could conquer the world had already broken down some time before, and finally she realised that the world she was pursuing, which she thought was her own and wanted to make understand her, which inspired her to break every rule made by her mother and father and oppose every word they said – that world considered her an outsider. With the naive eyes of her childhood she had not been able to see through the fine screen which concealed it. That world of nightclubs, discos, and the American boyfriends and girlfriends who were part of it, was actually governed by much stricter laws than her own home. From outside everything appeared glittering, fascinating and full of gaiety, but inside was hollow loneliness, obscenity, violence and murder.

At the time she'd begun to work at the nightclub she started living in Danny's apartment. Danny was an artist who made and sold silver jewelry. He was good looking, his personality was open and uninhibited. It was his whim to wear a beard and appear like a serious artist. He was also very often broke. He was addicted to every kind of consumable produce – tobacco, marijuana, LSD, and women. He used to say to Radhika, 'You're an Indian goddess. The sparks coming out of your body could set fire to anybody and reduce them to ash!'

'But the goddess doesn't set fire to anybody,' Radhika protested.

'Then who is it that burns everybody up? Oh, I remember, it's Shiva – his third eye. But how can you be Shiva? *I'm* Shiva.'

'The goddess is greater than Shiva. I learned from my mother how she keeps Shiva under her control.'

'Then I ought to be afraid of you. But you're not a goddess, you're a flower. You're so delicate and lovely you could wither just from the touch of a hand. But then, why does so much heat explode from you? What a strange combination of fire and flower! I've thought up a name for you, a name just as exotic as you – "fire-flower".'

146

One side of Danny's personality was that of the artist searching for beauty. But there was also in him a peculiar calculating tendency, to estimate the worth of everything he looked at. When Radhika came to live with him he started right off talking about sharing expenses equally. Her own financial situation was not very good so that after giving him her half of the household expenses she often didn't have enough left over to pay for her lunch. Everything was wasted on the disco, drugs and liquor.

Radhika's appearance excited Danny but he knew nothing at all about her inner world. Neither could touch the deepest level of feeling inside the other. Their relationship could not get beyond their lovemaking. When the novelty of Radhika's body had worn off, Danny tried to get her involved in group sex. Everybody getting together at night, round after round of drinks, and Radhika herself like some kind of plaything. Suddenly she felt completely isolated. While she looked for Danny's love in his romantic personality and amorous words, the fire-flower was gradually losing its glow.

Then the deepest hurt of all – Danny's open involvements with other women. Storms had come into Radhika's life at a very tender age. She wondered if she had been punishing herself just as a way to vent all her anger on her family. She began to long for home. This fellow Danny was completely separate, he belonged to a different world. The spontaneity with which he and his friends gave their bodies to one another was something Radhika could not cope with. She would have liked to destroy everything around her and escape, freeing herself from this labyrinth, and return to all those who were her own, whose love was free of any calculation, any trading in bodies. She yearned for the closeness to her mother, the liveliness and warmth of her sister and brother, the chance to sit at her father's bedside and share her mother's suffering.

Radhika felt as though someone had flayed her soul. She could not understand why her parents, her brother and sister, all hated her so much. Whatever she had done, had she done it deliberately? As though her father's stroke hadn't hurt her too! But it

147

was also possible that it was because of her that he had . . . She felt now as though the entire world had rejected her.

Scarcely aware of what she was doing, Radhika went on walking the dark streets until late at night, with Kanika's deadly denunciation echoing in her ears. Sometimes she saw her father lying helpless in the hospital, his eyes, frightfully distorted, glaring at her. Sometimes her mother's hurt eyes would reproach her. 'You're the cause of it! . . .'

Streets, alleyways, narrow roads, dark paths . . . Radhika kept walking but she had no idea where she was going, where she ought to go. While she had her wits about her she would never under any circumstances walk on those dark streets downtown. Today she was not even aware of them, the filth of these empty streets, the sidewalks covered with piles of garbage, a few homeless people strewn among them here and there. Sharp little nails were piercing her, heavy hammer blows, Kanika, Papa, Mummy, Danny . . . darkness, parking lots, warehouses, the sinister faces of age-old buildings. Inside Radhika how many volcanoes, fireflowers, all their sparks burning her up. She would become a sacrifice in her own fire, one scream of pain to terrorise the whole universe. How many had wounded her, how many times they'd trampled this fireflower, grabbed and torn it to its heart, shredded its petals, and sucked its nectar dry. A fireflower no more . . . you could call it a heap of ash.

The next morning people read in the newspapers that the body of a girl had been found near a parking lot. It appeared from the wounds on the corpse that a gang had beaten and raped her. The knife marks indicated that after raping her, if there had been any life left in her, the knives had finished the job.

Black blood congealed over the whole body, which was as stiff as tough wood. Blood flowing from uncounted wounds, swelling. Face so distorted you couldn't recognise it – such was the corpse Gita identified. But it wasn't Radhika, Gita thought as she fainted. But then – where was Radhika? Why had she scolded her so? She felt overwhelmed with remorse and guilt. So many thunderbolts all at once! Gita collapsed, as though someone had smashed every bone in her spine.

*

As she throws the offerings into the fire Guddo feels her fingers trembling. She tries to calm her mind by staring into the flames, but the trembling in her fingers won't stop. With her other hand she strokes them to steady them, without success. Eyes wet, lips trembling, she recites the *mantras* as she continues the sacrifice. *Om ayanta idhya atma jatavedas-stenedhyasva vardhasva ced casmana praiaya pasubhibrahya varcasenannadvena samadhyeya svaha* . . . Oh fire present in every object, this firewood is your spirit, through it be we illuminated, come forward and bring us forward, enrich us with progeny, beasts, material wealth and the divine light.

Everyone is present in Gita's house, observing mourning for Radhika. People's nagging nosey questions and observations devoid of sympathy . . . 'My dear, over here one has to keep a sharp eye on daughters, but why in the world was she out in the streets so late at night? She was working in a nightclub, but it wasn't anywhere near where they found her. God knows what happened. The poor girl met a very bad death, Gita can't accept that it's Radhika. Poor woman, she's taken it very hard. Just look, in a foreign country, like this . . . but anyway, Kanika's all right, she's a doctor now, she'll take care of everything . . . and then the son's already started college, fortunately.'

*

Ashok had brought his girlfriend with him and introduced her to Guddo. Her name was Amelia. Guddo thought how Radhika had never been able to bring her boyfriend home; if she had dared, Jijaji would have eaten her alive. What kind of people are we? she wondered, with one set of standards for daughters, another for sons. If Radhika had simply found acceptance in her own family this awful tragedy would not have happened.

A Panjabi lady who lived in Gita's building warned, 'Now you'd better see that Kanika's married. The sooner you get her off your hands, the better it will be. Who knows what these girls are up to? My relatives in India have a son who's got a great big house in Defence Colony. He finished his medical education two years ago, his family are fine people. Say the word and I'll write to them right away and set things in motion.'

So now a bridegroom for Kanika would be coming from Delhi too. But a marriage couldn't always set things right. Guddo was more than ever troubled by the tensions and complications besetting Anima and Rakesh. Anima was at a loose end; she still hadn't found a job. One place told her she had to have an MSc, not a PhD. So many years of hard work negated in a few minutes. There were no jobs to be found at her level of education – though Jane, Susan, everybody else had found high-paying jobs, only Anima couldn't get one. Rakesh's sarcasm burned her even more.

He often used to say, 'I ought to have married some girl with an MD too. We'd be living in clover. PhDs and all that are useless, it just means you can use your studies as an excuse to take a vacation from housework, on top of that, you don't earn any money either. So we lose on both counts.'

And Anima, hurt and miserable, would retort, 'Well just be grateful you found a job anyway. At least you didn't have to lose anything. Are you comparing me with my sister?'

'Who's comparing you with your sister? Did I say anything about her? But if Jane and Susan have found jobs, why haven't you? Either you haven't tried hard enough or there's something lacking – your personality . . .'

'Oh great, now you're starting to think there's something wrong with my personality! Are you having any trouble paying for the food to feed me?'

'Whether I do or not, you certainly are when it comes to cooking it.'

'It's because of this house I haven't found any work. When I was finally offered a job outside the city you wouldn't let me take it. You keep me so tied up in the house that I can't give enough attention to what I should be doing. When I wanted to go to Chicago you said, "If we have to maintain two households what's the point of being married?" All you care about is getting ahead for yourself. What did you ever do for me?'

'I understand,' said Rakesh bitterly. 'You arranged for me to get my green card, then your mother spoke to her boyfriend and had him give me this job, so now shouldn't I be so grateful that I ought to remain under your thumb? Whatever way the mother and daughter arrange things, I'm just supposed to accept it.'

Anima could not bear to hear her mother insulted. And now it was clear, Rakesh didn't have the least respect even for her mother. How could he dare use that word 'boyfriend' for Uncle Juneja? Flaring up, she said, 'You're going too far. Say whatever you like to me but why bring Mummy into it? When you do you just show how crude you are, it doesn't make you look any better. If you think so little of me, why were you so hot to marry me?'

This was another assault on Rakesh in the matter of his green card. His anger exploded inside him like a volcano, sending lava not only into his words but into his hands as well:

'You're low, you're rotten! How dare you insult me like that!'

His hands kept moving. Slap after slap, striking, punching . . .

Full of misgivings when she saw her daughter's red swollen eyes, Guddo barely found the courage to ask her what had happened.

'I've left Rakesh. I can't stay there any longer. Every day we fight over something or other and he beats me, just look . . .'

Guddo stared at the black-and-blue bruises Anima showed her on her back, arms, and ribs.

She was speechless with shock. She had always thought that anyone who had the ability to become a doctor would of necessity also have some common humanity and decency. But what she was seeing now . . . Could Rakesh be so insensitive, so harsh and childish? Still, she could not imagine Anima divorcing him. She said, 'I'll call Rakesh and talk to him. Brutality like this . . .'

Anima interrupted her, 'You're not going to phone him. I intend to talk to a lawyer right away.'

'But why have you decided so quickly that divorce is the right solution? Don't do anything foolish! I'll make Rakesh understand – '

151

'If you try, it will just make things even worse. I'm the one who's had to live with him, not you.'

'Do you realise how difficult it will be for you to live alone? It seems easy enough to say "divorce". But I've seen girls go from bad to worse after a divorce.'

'Mummy, is Najma happy or sad now that she's divorced? I'm just as strong as she is. What difference does it make anyway if you're married or not? People can be happy living alone too. Why is a woman compelled to spend her life with a man?'

'But for a woman nothing works out right without a man. There's no place in society for a woman alone. Haven't you seen what it's been like for me?'

'Mummy, it's looking at you that gives me courage. The way you've been able to do everything on your own with confidence in yourself – that makes me realise I can do something under my own power too. Most of all, why should I have to put up with a marriage that's been such torture for me?'

'But Anima – '

'I realise that in your society divorce is considered disreputable, but should I sacrifice myself out of fear of being disreputable?'

Guddo kept silent. She could not calm the storm raging inside Anima. She would forget the wounds to her body but not those to her spirit. Too many times Rakesh's sharp taunts had bloodied her soul. Communication between them had come to an end. Battling over everything, stopping only after insults and beatings. Nor could she any longer hide the troubles in her home from those around her.

Jane gave her opinion. 'When a husband doesn't respect you and won't consider you equal, why should you have to stay with him? How can anybody beat another person so savagely? I wonder if you realise you can go to the police and have him arrested for beating you like that. In this country nobody has the right to treat a woman that way.'

Anima burst into tears.

'My mother says that once you're married you have to make a

152

go of it no matter what. Whether it makes you cry or suffer . . . whatever the situation.'

Then Najma said, 'There's no need to be such a martyr. What are you afraid of? You're self-reliant, how can you stand for anybody to tyrannise over you? It's you women yourselves who don't want to free yourselves from the marriage trap. Why hesitate? You can stay with me until you find a job. Apply for a post-graduate fellowship right away, there are loads of them in chemistry. And please don't go to your mother, she'll only talk you into going back to that brute and starting your relationship all over again.'

Anima was frightened. What if she was making a mistake? She was still standing at the very threshold of life, and already she might be losing everything and have to regret it for the rest of her life. Did Rakesh and his love amount to nothing more than the coming together of two bodies? But really, if love had been able to grow between them there could not have been all the fighting, the stinging sarcasm and insults, the beatings. This couldn't be what her life was meant to be, she simply could no longer follow her mother's directions. Anyway, there was no reason for them to share the same point of view. Why should people be able to make her do things which wouldn't work, and who were they anyway? Aunt Gita, Aunt Pinki, Rakesh. Why couldn't they accept what was right for Anima? Everybody was concerned with himself. And her mother – worrying for nothing about Indian society here . . . and afraid of lies, of Anima getting too old for marrying, not finding the right bridegroom . . . But feeling desperate, Guddo had arranged the marriage in a hurry. When she should have waited till now. No, she thought Anima would have been too old – as though a woman's beauty was gone by the time she was twenty-eight. So Guddo had not let her do anything she wanted.

While Rakesh was on duty at the hospital, Anima packed and moved to Najma's. From there she called Guddo. 'Mummy, it was a mistake for me to keep going home to you and letting you just send me back to him. I didn't realise that it was up to me alone to run my life. I won't go back to him any more.'

Guddo's heart sank. What were all these things happening around her? Who had spoiled her sacrificial offering? For just one bit of happiness how much happiness had to be sacrificed . . . Oh Lord, don't ruin my offering . . . and don't inflict ruin on the sacrificer . . . *Yatkamaste juhumastanno astu vayam patayo rayinam.* Whatever we desire, fulfill our wishes . . .

Twenty-eight

As soon as he got his degree in computer science Raju found a job with a well-established company. There was a big demand for computer experts, and furthermore, Raju's work was of high quality. Now Guddo would be able to buy herself a fine house, for he was getting an excellent salary. But still, he did not appear content.

She could not understand why he was in such low spirits. When he came home he would throw himself down on the bed and lie there. Saying nothing, keeping to himself, giving no answer. Guddo would shake him and say, 'Why don't you speak to me, why won't you tell me anything?'

'Please, mother, leave me alone. The office routine really tires me out, it's so boring, always the same work from morning to night. I'm totally exhausted.'

'I thought you liked your work.'

'I don't know . . . everything in that office seems meaningless. As though I didn't exist . . . working like a machine from nine to five, that's all . . . other people exactly like me . . .'

'Then what are you going to do?'

Raju yawned and said in a low voice, 'I can't tell you, mother, I don't know myself. But I think I've got to do something else, something really important.'

Just then Arun dropped by. 'Raju, my friend,' he said, 'why are you flaked out on your bed at seven in the evening? Up, up! Let's go out and have some fun. In this country the city's just coming to life at night. I brought the taxi so I can get in a little work too, then we'll go to a bar and hang out.'

155

When Arun dropped Raju off at home that night it was after two.

Guddo had been worried. Now, when he came in, she could smell something peculiar on Raju's breath, something she'd never smelled before. Her young son was a man earning his own way – Guddo, still traditional, did not think it proper to question him. But that strange smell coming from Raju's mouth was like one more poisonous attack on Guddo's heart. Perplexed, she could only stare at Raju.

The moment Guddo lay down the telephone rang. It was Pinki, asking in a worried voice, 'Didn't Arjun come by your place?'

'Why – hasn't he come home yet?'

'I don't know what's happened, he's always come in late, but tonight is the latest ever.'

Arjun was not at all like his cousins Raju and Ashok, maybe, Guddo sometimes thought, because he'd been brought up in that part of Manhattan called Greenwich Village which was considered bohemian. Not only from the time he started school but even before in the daycare centre his friendships had been only with the American children around him. They studied together, played together, and he later became a star on the local football team. Tall, robust, fair – with his Haryana heritage he fitted in perfectly in this American environment. His way of speaking, his movements and gestures and expressions were all exactly like those of American boys. He preferred the company of his American friends to that of his cousins, who seemed to him to be of a different breed; his tastes did not accord with theirs, nor did he feel any identification, any spontaneous link with them. For her part, Pinki wanted him to have some acquaintance with his Indian language, customs and traditions, so in the beginning she liked having her sisters around, and now there was her mother-in-law with them too. But though he learned a little Hindi from his grandmother, he and his cousins usually spoke in English.

Arjun's parents did not want for anything, and he was given as much money as he could spend – an only son with parents earning good salaries. From the time he started high school he wasn't restricted in any way. Pinki and Satinder were liberal by nature and did not object no matter how late Arjun stayed out with his friends. On the few occasions when Pinki did speak about it Arjun said, 'Mom, sometimes the games go on a long time. Afterwards we all sit around having something to eat and rapping, so of course it gets late.'

Around the house everything was lively and brilliantly lit all night long, the neighbourhood bars and nightclubs stayed open until three or four o'clock in the morning, and there were always people in the streets, so Pinki tended not to worry very much.

Arjun was also intelligent and sensible. When he studied his grades were excellent, when he didn't they might drop a little but there was never any question of his failing. He was interested in lots of different things. Satinder said:

'It's all right, he ought to develop an all-round personality rather than stay glued to his books like Raju.'

Satinder had given up trying to mould Arjun in his own image and style; he felt that having too many rules would only make him rebellious or impede his development. So Satinder believed less and less in interfering in his son's life.

Pinki was distressed. 'When a boy gets older it's no longer his mother's place to supervise him,' she told her husband. 'But you're always busy with your books, you have no idea where the boy is going . . .'

This night she had telephoned all Arjun's friends. One said that Arjun had gone to a bar. Satinder was alarmed. Which bar? Tonight all kinds of fears suddenly sprang up in his mind: maybe Arjun had been beaten up by a gang; he was a strongly built boy but faced with a gang he might have to run and hide . . . or maybe now he too was a member of a gang. These thoughts distressed Satinder, but he consoled himself, remembering that Arjun was not a stranger in this environment, this was his own country, his own society, he was at home here.

The phone rang: a friend of Arjun's. Arjun was lying unconscious in a gay bar from an overdose of drugs. Pinki and Satinder, dressed as they were threw on coats and rushed out. The bar was

157

not far away. In her distress Pinki was in a cold sweat, a sour taste was in her mouth. After they found him they checked him in at the emergency room of a nearby hospital. He was brought to a room where Pinki sat all night by his bed, racked by every kind of fear and praying for his recovery.

The doctor advised her that it would be necessary to have Arjun examined by a psychologist who might cure of him of his drug habit.

As though that were not enough, Pinki was destined to suffer another thunderbolt. The psychologist took her and Satinder apart and said, 'I presume you realise that your son is homosexual.'

For Pinki it was as though Arjun had been diagnosed as having a dangerous, incurable, life-threatening disease. This was no longer her son – he had become some sort of alien creature. As soon as she thought of him her head began to swim and, feeling helpless, she sobbed with the pain of it. She said, 'But he's still terribly young, doctor. Sexual suppression can take this form, can't it? Afterwards as he goes along he'll become normal, won't he?'

The doctor either had no definite answer or did not want to give one. Pinki said to Satinder, 'When the two of us are all right how can Arjun be like that? I won't accept that he'll stay this way when he's grown up. Listen, don't say anything to your mother, she's always dreaming of finding a bride for Arjun and the grand wedding he's going to have.'

The very thought made her heart beat violently, she felt a twisting in her stomach. Satinder stroked her forehead and said:

'Why torment yourself? If he's normal, fine, if not, well, he has a right to lead his life in his own way. You regard marriage and having children as the only possible fulfilment for a man, but there are many other means by which to create . . . a writer's books, an artist's paintings, a scientist's discoveries. You ought to be his helper in whatever he wants to do or make of his life. Don't fight it. After all, remember, a lot of the world's greatest artists have been homosexual.'

Pinki was not consoled. 'I don't know why everything seems so dark all around me,' she said, bursting into sobs again.

When she was alone with Arjun, she asked, 'Do you really feel that you're . . . different from others?'

Humiliated by her question Arjun could only answer, 'I know how you feel, Mom, some of my friends have parents who don't understand them. I can't help it.'

And still Pinki wanted to understand, she kept trying and trying to feel what it must be like – why couldn't she? Her own son was turning into a person outside the sphere of her experience. What difference was this going to make in her daily life at home? The kind of life which Pinki herself had lived, or everything she had imagined for her son's life, would now amount to nothing at all.

While Satinder, interpreting everything from an intellectual point of view, found an explanation for every accident, each great reversal, all the calamities, or else simply accepted them, Pinki was not capable of such a rational approach. Reasoning couldn't save her from the guilt which now haunted her. She herself had been raised in a big family, scarcely ever spending a day completely alone. But she had given Arjun such an empty, lonely home. What could have happened inside the child? No companionship, no friendship, no communication, Mom and Dad always very busy . . . so he went looking for his world outside. Lots of friends out there . . . and lots of fun with those friends . . . the house empty, why come home? So he stayed out later and later. The doctor told her that children attracted to drugs often felt themselves very isolated and neglected at home. Arjun was not a rejected child by any means, but rather a spoiled only son . . . Inside Pinki a stream of silent tears kept flowing.

Satinder said they should have a party: Pinki's great dream had been realised – from the first of next month she was going to be the director of her own library. But Pinki's enthusiasm had died. She said:

'Should I resign? After so many sacrifices to get that position, who knows how many more I'll have to make to hold on to it.'

'Don't be silly.'

But after this he said nothing more.

Twenty-nine

Both Tanima and Anuj were obsessed with furthering their careers. Guddo said to Tanima:

'Don't even think of trying to have another child now. You're terribly run down. Just keep busy with your work.'

For Tanima sickness, medicines, and instruments day and night. Anuj was specialising in two areas; he'd now finished general medicine and would do surgery next. He felt he had to get ahead any way he could. There were no girls phoning him at home now. Whether or not they quarrelled or Tanima's ego was hurt, everything was being done very rationally and deliberately. The two had much to share between them. During the year college friends, doctors looking for jobs, came to visit and they'd stay for days. Tanima said:

'With all these guests don't you think we ought to have a house?'

'Hold it!' said Anuj. 'There's no need to spend a lot of money for a house just yet, we can get along perfectly well in the apartment. When we've saved up enough money we'll open up a first-class clinic of our own. The real earnings are in practice, hospital work brings in a limited income.'

Guddo asked, 'Are you taking a house? Have you decided to settle in this country then?'

'What else? What is there for us in India?'

'That's true, but you used to say, didn't you, that you'd go back to Chandigarh and open a nursing home in Papa's name?'

'Oh, that! . . .' Tanima had forgotten. 'That was an old dream, far away and long ago. It would be very hard to go back to India

161

and stay there now. In my whole life I couldn't earn as much as I do here in a year. The hospital environment is a lot healthier here too, everything's so clean. And then, all of you are here too. When we're old, then we'll see . . .'

Judy's distress could be heard in her voice over the telephone. Arun had been arrested and taken away. The police had discovered drugs on him. Judy never suspected that he'd ever been involved with them before, she said, he'd kept her in the dark. The police had questioned her at length, she had no idea what to do. 'You know him so well, Guddo, he wouldn't do anything like that, would he?'

Guddo wondered why Arun would try to make a profit selling drugs when his earnings were already sufficient for him. She worried that if Judy learned about the bride waiting in India there was no telling how much she would suffer. But fortunately Arun probably hadn't yet completed arrangements for the bride, and he'd even spoken about paying a lump sum to annul the marriage.

Judy was running about in a panic. She had to get Arun released – she must put up his bail . . . some customer must have left the drugs in his taxi . . . he'd been arrested without cause . . . her Arun was a decent fellow, he had nothing to do with such things, Judy was sure of it.

When finally he was released, Guddo said to him:

'The way Judy's suffered on your account you ought to have married her ten times, not once.'

Arun smiled.

'I can't understand your coldness! The poor girl is even trying to learn Hindi. You've seen how perfectly she wears a sari. How much more Indian do you want to make her?'

'Well, she can't become Indian, especially in the eyes of my mother and father.'

'And in yours?'

'As far as I'm concerned that's not what's important. To tell the truth, Didi, I'm more and more doubtful. From the very beginning I've felt a great obligation to Judy. She's been my patron, my saviour. And I'm just crushed under the weight of all that obligation. Sometimes I ask myself, "Do I love Judy and do I really want to be married to her?" I wonder, is my relationship with Judy just a matter of convenience or do I really . . .'

'Arun, all I can say is this: the way you depend on Judy I don't see how, if you want to stay in this country, you can do it without her. But you know yourself better than I do.'

Arun abruptly changed the subject. 'I haven't seen Raju for some time – where is he?'

She answered only, 'If you take him with you again don't stay out so late.'

Guddo fretted constantly because of Raju. Her son was everything to her and she trembled for fear some harm might come to him. Why was he so depressed, so alone and introverted? Today he hadn't even gone to the office. She asked him why.

'No idea, didn't feel like it . . . I can't go on earning money just for the sake of money. I don't know what I want to do . . . but something else, I want something else.'

'But do you know what it is?'

'I can't quite get it into focus, nothing looks clear. Can I ask you something? Is wealth a means to get somewhere or is it an end in itself?'

'What do you think?'

'I can't figure it out. It seems that I've no real aim in life.'

Guddo was afraid. Trying to console him, she said, 'The aim of one's life is, well, to live it truly in one's own way.'

'But what is the way to live your life?'

'You can't expect a single answer to a question like that. There isn't any one way. Everybody understands the question in his own way.'

'But what's *your* way?'

Guddo remained silent a little while, then carefully putting the words together she said, 'The centre of my life is you three children. Every important decision I've ever made has been directed toward your welfare.'

'I don't have anything like that to centre my life on.'

'Your career, Raju! At your age your career ought to be foremost.'

'That's a very long, boring road.'

'What are you talking about? If you don't make a career for yourself what are you going to do? How can you build a life without it? Have you thought of something else?'

'So far I haven't thought of anything, I haven't understood anything. Sometimes I think I'll earn such piles of money that I'll become a very powerful person just on the strength of my money. And sometimes the career ... money is the most repulsive of all, just boring boring boring!'

Thirty

Burning steadily in the *havan* the pieces of wood seem like coals, and some of them have already turned to ash.

*

Juneja said, 'Why worry so much about Raju? After he's settled down to work for a few more years see that he's married. Everything's sure to turn out fine. Now just stop fretting and look to your own life. You're always so busy there's never time for us to meet any more.'

'I used to think that once the girls were married I'd be free of worry,' said Guddo. 'But now I've got three or four times the responsibilities I used to have.'

'Look, everything's going to work out, but you need some discipline to make yourself take a bit of time off. This country's law is, earn for five days, spend and shop for the house for one day, and one day just for pleasure. So tell me now, which is your day for pleasure?'

'But in this country the day is divided into three parts. Eight hours at the office, eight at home and eight for sleeping. But tell me, who can manage the office part in only eight hours? You need two or two and a half hours just for commuting, and then there's overtime. So tell me, on which day do you stop work after eight hours?'

They both laughed. Guddo went on, 'The fact is, it's impossible to keep a true balance in dividing up the time. Like when you lose your balance if you have a foot in one boat and one foot in another.'

'Two boats? Why not three? All right, now tell me when we can meet.'

'My daughters, Raju . . . there's always some complication to sort out with one of the three. Some time or other I'll drop in at your office.'

In Guddo's busy life her involvement with Juneja was beginning to seem unimportant. Finally she was becoming aware of the meaning of her relationship with him: now that all the children were secure in their jobs it made little difference whether she saw him or not. At one point her feelings toward him had actually soured; this was when, after Tanima had completed two years of her residency, her contract had suddenly been terminated. Dr Juneja had flatly refused to help. He explained that at this point he could not jeopardise his own position. That was all her two years' work in his hospital amounted to. Afterwards she was lucky enough to find a post in another hospital without any help from him. Well, Guddo thought, Juneja's finished doing what he was needed for.

But then she felt like getting together with him once more. She could share her troubles with him, it had been essential to bring him all her problems, whether he had any solution for them or not.

One day, without phoning in advance, on a whim she went to Juneja's office. His secretary told her that at this moment he could not see her. When word was sent to him, even then she was made to wait. Nothing like this had ever happened before, she'd always been given what he called 'top priority'. Some time later she saw an expensively dressed Indian woman emerge from his office. She had once seen this same woman with Juneja outside that French restaurant where he had brought Guddo the first time they went out. Guddo now began to understand quite a few things more clearly. Suddenly depressed, she had no desire to confront Juneja now. She felt tears fill her eyes. It was all coming to an end perfectly naturally – but had it been anything in the first place?

'You may go in now, Mrs Chaddha, the doctor's free.'

Guddo wanted to say it was now too late, she had to leave. But her feet were already moving toward Juneja's room.

'Come in, Mrs Chaddha,' he said, and after Guddo closed the door behind her, 'How are you, Uma?'

Exercising all her self-control, Guddo said, 'We haven't spoken for a long time, so since I was just passing by I thought I'd say hello.'

'I'm glad you did. Please have a seat.' While he spoke Juneja kept his eyes fixed on some papers on his desk.

After sitting in silence for some time Guddo managed to speak again:

'I guess you're very busy?'

'No, no, it was just that I had to look these papers over and sign them. The office work never ends, you know. It's really rather like running a household. You always have things to do and – there it is, you just keep on doing them. Endless work. Even if you don't do it things keep moving along. Now if Indira Gandhi just sat around and did nothing about the country's problems the country wouldn't come to a stop, would it, but if she did, well . . . It's all a question of management, whether it's the home, the office or the country.'

It seemed to Guddo that Juneja was chattering this way just to keep some distance between them. She was more annoyed than ever and felt that she had nothing at all to say to him. She stood up and said, 'I better be going now.'

'Why? Sit down, please. Won't you have some coffee?'

'No, I don't care for any.'

Guddo quickly left the room without looking at Juneja's face. She was fuming. But why? . . . there wasn't any kind of real bond between them . . . in that nameless relationship there was no place at all for rights or complaining . . . a commonplace affair . . . neither promises nor expectations . . . but then why this piercing hurt, this sense of betrayal? She didn't feel up to walking to the train station, so she sat on a park bench outside the hospital and tried to control her tears.

What had happened? For such a long time she had been keeping Juneja at a distance. She had neither telephoned him

167

nor, when she came, made any excuse for not being able to talk with him. But this is the way relationships sometimes fell apart . . .

'Mrs Chaddha! Uma! What are you doing here? Good heavens, how pale you are!'

When she looked up there was Juneja. 'I was just going to the garage to get my car,' he went on. 'When I caught sight of you in the distance I couldn't believe it. Come along now, let me drive you home, it's starting to get dark.'

Guddo felt too weak to say anything. She got up and walked with him in silence.

It was beyond her capacity now either to break off or get back together with him. As though every relationship was like a kind of rubber band . . . you pull and stretch and it goes back to its original shape. But if you really apply a lot of force even a rubber band breaks. She wondered if she was strong enough to do it.

Thirty-one

A dreary rainy Sunday. The shapes of raindrops seemed to be printed on the dirty windowpanes, the fog outside brought its darkness into the room. Guddo wondered what she was living for now. The children had made their own lives. Of what use was she any more? She had no idea where Raju was these days . . . with Tanima and Anuj it was nothing but work and more work . . . Anima had started her post-doctoral research. Pinki said:

'Sister, it's time for you to remarry. I know an American woman who married when she was sixty. You ought to have a companion at this point in life, someone the same age. The children have made their own lives, you can't keep relying on them . . .'

Guddo's face was distorted with her frown.

Everybody said the same thing – there were no obstacles, you should remarry. So you think I haven't married because of some superficial embarrassment or shame. True, the children used to be a reason . . . But there's a much bigger reason – myself!

A kind of ache started up inside Guddo. How much she had missed in life, how much she'd given up, how many desires she had failed to satisfy . . . every day a dream of returning . . . and every day a morning of hard work.

Guddo's reflections were broken by the ringing of the telephone.

'Mrs Chaddha? This is Batra speaking. I'm calling from the airport.'

For a few moments Guddo was bewildered.

'Who . . . the lawyer . . . you?'

'Yes, I didn't have a chance to let you know in advance so of course you're surprised. Actually, I had to come all of a sudden because of a business deal. I still had your address and phone number so I thought I'd give you a ring when I got here.'

Guddo could think of nothing to say but 'Yes, of course . . .'

'So the thing is, I'll get a taxi and come straight over to your place. How far away from here are you? Is there a bus that goes that way?'

Guddo explained how to get there. Afterwards she dashed around, putting the house in order. She had been idle since morning and not yet bathed, but there was no time now. She hastily washed her hands and face and put on a sari, arranged her hair, applied lipstick and a *bindi*, and quickly inspected herself in the mirror. Then she gathered up the heavy Sunday newspapers and stacked them neatly. The table and chairs were dusty. Now that Lawyer Batra was coming to stay some time in the house every corner had to be spotless. Bathroom, closets. As quickly as she could Guddo started putting the kitchen in order, then, remembering the living room, broke off before she'd finished straightening it out. She consoled herself with the thought that there was a lot of traffic on the road from the airport so that it would be some time yet before he arrived and she'd still have a few more moments after all to get herself and the house in shape.

She regretted not having had some advance notice so that she could have arranged everything properly. After so many years, here was an old friend coming to see her! After her daughters were married she had not returned again to India. What would have become of Batra during this time, what would he be like? And would his wife know that he was planning to stay with Guddo? Unless, God forbid, she was with him . . .

In another forty-five minutes Batra reached the apartment.

'Well, Mrs Chaddha! You didn't invite me but I've come anyway.'

Guddo wasn't sure whether he was teasing or just expressing his pleasure at seeing her, but she was impatient to learn what he had really come for. He explained right away that the son of one of his clients had been working as an engineer in Texas. He had divorced his wife and, fearing that custody of their child would surely go to her, he had taken the child back to India. Then his ex-wife had brought a charge of kidnapping against him so of course he was concerned that he would be arrested the moment he came back to America and he was afraid his job was in jeopardy too.

'So I've come to represent him in this case,' Batra continued. 'From here I have to go first to Boston, then to Texas. On my way back I'll stop over in New York again.'

Guddo was proud to think that Batra was so respected as a lawyer that people were ready to spend a lot of money sending him to America.

'Enough of business, Mrs Chaddha. Whether you remember me or not, I certainly remember you.' Saying this, he threw his arms out and embraced Guddo. Before she could break away his right hand was already pressing against her breasts and his lips were on hers.

'Please,' Guddo said, 'I can't breathe.'

She managed to free her mouth, then gradually pushed his hand away. 'What in the world's happened to you?' she said. 'Sit over there and calm down! After all these years we have lots of news to exchange.'

'That can all wait,' said Lawyer Batra. At once he grabbed her again and assaulted her with kisses. 'You have no idea how I've been longing for you through the years!' Saying this he flung her down on the sofa and threw the full weight of his body on her.

Hospitality, courtesy, respect for a relationship that went back years, so much gratitude for his past help – Guddo's mind was overwhelmed with confusion. Should she try to shove him away or submit? Perhaps there was still some pleasure to be had, some suppressed desire in herself . . . there weren't many left who would desire this body, nor would it long remain worth enjoying . . . So then, whatever happened . . . Guddo's body, so long bound fast in its repressions, gradually began to open. As he unfastened the buttons of her blouse, Batra said:

171

'Hurrah! Your breasts are as firm as a virgin girl's.'

Guddo knew these words were meant to praise her but they struck her as cheap and vulgar. She shoved him away. He was disappointed but this time accepted her rejection, though she knew it was only a temporary escape for her.

The next morning, when Batra had to leave for Boston, Guddo breathed with relief. But not long after he'd gone his daughter Mita appeared on her doorstep. She looked very pregnant.

'When did you come over?' Guddo asked her, handing her a plate with some cheesecake on it. 'And what are you here for? I had no idea . . . Mr Batra made no mention at all. Is your husband with you?'

'I flew over a week ago. Anil's still in India. I've been staying with a girlfriend in New Jersey. If you won't mind, Auntie, I'd like to come and stay here a while.'

'Of course, of course, stay by all means. The apartment is empty now, even Raju doesn't come home any more these days, so it will be nice for me.'

'Fine then, I'll come to stay on Monday.'

On Friday Mita called Guddo at her office. She asked right away, 'Auntie, how much does it cost to have a baby in America?'

'Why? You're not thinking of having it here, are you?'

'No, but, well, I don't know . . . maybe I will. The doctor set the date at the twenty-sixth of next month. But I might be going back at the end of this month.'

'Won't that be too late to go back? Will the doctor let you travel?'

'Yes, I've just come, you know. The doctor didn't say anything about it.'

'Have you spoken to a doctor here?'

'No, I haven't. The thing is, Anil said that if I had the baby in America it would automatically be an American citizen. Then when he's eighteen he could bring us over here. If you don't have some close relative it's just about impossible to come and live here.'

Guddo was astonished by this reasoning. 'Oh,' she said, 'you people certainly make plans far in advance!'

Embarrassed, Mita said, 'What else can we do, Auntie? Conditions in India are getting worse day by day. You can't imagine how hard it's going to be for our children to find work. If another door opens up to them, well . . . Whatever we can do . . .'

Guddo could not help laughing. Whether the child wanted it or not, these parents were going to use him to their advantage as much as possible. For the next eighteen years this key to the future was sure to be treated with the greatest affection and care, he would be his parents' prize investment.

Guddo said, 'It will cost at least ten thousand dollars.'

'But Auntie, couldn't Tanima deliver the child?'

Guddo was alarmed. So Mita's intention was to stay with her or Tanima while she had the baby.

'Tanima isn't an obstetrician, Mita. And you won't get a free delivery just on her say-so. That will be true for the whole procedure. Do you have medical insurance?'

'No . . . but that can be arranged.'

'Mita, if you'd written me from India and asked me if something could be done . . . No delivery is easy, after all. We're all working, and you'll have to have somebody to look after you.'

'You don't have to worry about it, I haven't made any decision yet, I was just asking.' With that Mita hung up.

Then Guddo phoned Batra in Boston.

'You didn't tell me that Mita was over here just now.'

'Yes, her travel agency got her a ticket that was practically free so she decided to come. But you sound upset about it – why?'

'No, no, I'm not upset at all, just surprised that you didn't mention it.' Silence at the other end of the line. Then Guddo brought up the real question:

'Did Mita come here to have her baby?'

'No, nothing like that. Well, she did say that if that were possible her husband was thinking of coming over too to look for work here.'

'But won't it be difficult? A first child, and there could be complications. If it's a Caesarean it will also cost a lot more.'

173

It seemed that Batra was not pleased to hear all this. 'My dear,' he said, 'why are you worrying about it? She didn't mean to impose on you, and we're certainly not going to force you into anything. If you want to do something, well . . . otherwise . . .'

His tone seemed to be telling her: I'm testing you to find out if *you* are willing to do something for *us* or not.

Guddo felt as though Batra had reappeared from some earlier incarnation squatting on her doorstep to collect the interest on an old loan. What could she do? It wouldn't do to make the lawyer angry. In how many Indian contexts certain requirements continued to be in force even now! There was always one thing or another. Batra managed all her business over there. Whether to make her tenants cough up their rent, or evict them, or if somebody needed some documents, a certificate or anything else. Obviously, she herself couldn't go to India every day, she had to have some trusted crony on the spot. So it wouldn't do now for him to go away angry.

But a few days later Batra telephoned. There was no mention of Mita. He said he was terribly bored in Boston. 'They're giving me just a hundred dollars a week for hotel and food. These Indian bastards aren't capable of shedding their Indian hide. Back in India they tell me they're earning millions here. Establish your practice in America, they say, and you'll get a lot of important Indian clients to get started. But the bastards I've met are all spongers . . . friends or relatives of somebody or other. They don't have any idea that this lawyer has to eat too. So I'm going to start making approaches to some American company . . .'

Speaking with all the sweetness she could muster, Guddo said, 'Mr Batra, why are you so upset? Come back to New York, a change of air will do you good.'

He welcomed the invitation. 'Maybe you're right. I'll try to come this weekend. I'm really very tired of Boston.'

On Saturday evening Batra came back from Boston. After they chatted a while he asked:

'Raju hasn't put in an appearance – where is he?'

'He does whatever he feels like doing. He's gone out some-where with Arun for the weekend.'

Batra had gradually unbuttoned his shirt half-way down. He moved closer and began to pass his hands over Guddo's shoulder. The hands quickly glided down and touched her breasts. But then, to her relief, he drew a little apart and said:

'Mrs Chaddha, I'd like to settle here too for a while. Could you be of any help to me?'

Guddo was stunned. 'But what can you do here? You have your practice well established over there. The law is different here too, and then there's a lot of competition in the legal profession.'

The lawyer's enthusiasm was not diminished. He said, 'The person I've come over to represent in America told me he'll see that I get some more cases, then I'll also try on my own. Right now there's a flood of Indians coming in.'

Guddo made another effort. 'But then, you know, there isn't that much work to assure a constant income, and then, there's your household in India.'

'All true, but just see, I'll do a little law study in this country. I can stay here, away from my family for a whole year – they have enough money to get along, and anyway, what kind of elaborate housekeeping is there, with only two children? I can send something from here too. So could you help me a bit in connection with my studies?'

Guddo realised that the lawyer was serious about wanting to start studying all over again at the age of fifty – and bring his whole family to America. Did she then – a clerk-accountant living far from the city in a rent-controlled apartment costing three hundred dollars a month – appear like a 'successful' resident of the new land?

And then, if all the people connected with her memories of India should come here, what would be left for her to return to back home?

Just to think of it made Guddo wretched.

'Look, I'll do whatever I can. But you don't even have a work

175

permit, you know. They're very strict about that these days. If they find out they fine the employer for giving work to illegal aliens. So no one's willing to hire anybody who doesn't have a permit.'

'Don't worry about that, Mrs Chaddha, I'll figure out something or other. But if I could stay here while I'm studying in New York . . .'

Guddo tried to put him off. 'I'll have to ask Raju – this is his home now. I can't imagine what the children will think about your staying here . . . And Raju isn't married yet, so it's important to keep up appearances.'

Batra drew closer. His hands began to move, tracing the outline of Guddo's body.

'But you're free now, Mrs Chaddha,' he said. 'Your children are all settled. Now your life is your own. You should live it the way you want, but you're still tied to the children. Enough! Your days of sacrifice and austerity are finished.'

And as he spoke he came so close that his breath clashed with hers, her breasts touched the hair on his chest. Suddenly something happened to Guddo, just what she never knew, but with both her hands she shoved Batra's body away as it was about to fall over hers and stepped back to stand facing him. She was panting but she managed to put her words together with deliberation:

'Did you think that when I moved here I became someone else and my values, my standards all changed? In India you never would have dared but you come here into my house and assault me. I've tried to be courteous and show you respect, but all you really thought was that living here had changed me. When I talked about freedom you thought it just meant physical independence. Every Indian man I meet thinks that because I'm living in America I must have turned into a whore. Just like you now. But listen, whatever earth and bone I'm made of is still the same, and I've given it to my children too. I may not know what's right or wrong but I know this much, my daughters are living their lives honestly and honourably, the way I taught them according to Indian standards and Indian morality. And just wait and see

176

the kind of Indian girl of good family my son's going to marry. My own sisters' children have strayed from the true path in this society, but I didn't let it happen to mine. And now you . . . you want to sully the purity of my home – but it's never going to happen. Now get out.'

Guddo felt as though every cell in her body, every atom of the apartment, had been dishonoured, and she would never be able to wash them clean again. The apartment would have to be purified, so too this soul, this body . . . Her mother did the fire sacrifice for every kind of purification. She remembered how every time one of the children recovered from smallpox her mother performed the *havan* to cleanse the air.

Confused and angry, Batra said, 'Mrs Chaddha,' but Guddo interrupted him:

'No, Mr Batra, sitting over there in India you haven't understood anything at all about your countrymen living abroad. India flows along at its own speed, going forward or becoming modern, but we haven't moved beyond the point where we were when we left it to come here. Even if dating for boys and girls has become socially acceptable in India, I've built my children's lives on the traditions and social restrictions which I knew in my time. You know that time is moving ahead in India, but our time has stopped right where it was. Our present and our future are built on the India of our past.

'You've seen the temples and *gurdvaras* being built every day here in America – tell me where in India so much money is spent on building temples. Indians there sit around thinking of newer and newer industries and factories to start, and at home here we beat the drum for *dharma*, standards and tradition. You may call it our insecurity, or say we're trying to recapture what we're losing, or have already lost, by means of our temples. Even if we're seen wearing slacks or skirts, what we wear inside us stays the same. We don't change ourselves. Wherever we go we create our own India again, whether others think it's bad or good, even if where we live is called a ghetto or Little India, even if because of our closed society later generations are kicked out of their adopted countries, or whatever price we have to pay.'

177

'Mrs Chaddha, I can't make any sense of what you're saying. You left your country of your own free will and came here. I can't see the point of breaking away from so much and adopting a whole new way of living if you try to keep your children as Indian as possible. I suspect that what you're saying really isn't true for you either.'

'Who's talking about true or false? Was Trishanku right or wrong? Anyone who hasn't climbed up on the heights like him has no idea of what empty space is like. Or how can anyone who hasn't dangled in empty space free himself of his doubts as to whether movement is in going up or coming back down? And because it's impossible for him to do either one his fate is pain and discontent, and to get free of it he'll sometimes run this way, sometimes another, sometimes he'll build temples and sometimes a clinic and then wherever salvation is . . .'

She had spoken with such emotion that she felt exhausted and shut her eyes. The next day Batra left for Texas.

Thirty-two

Outside the sky was covered with layer after layer of dense clouds. The storm hadn't let up. Sharp gusts of howling wind violently rattled the closed doors and windowpanes. Guddo had fallen asleep watching the news about the storm on television. When she woke up in the middle of the night she began at once to worry. Where was Raju?

Not in bed, though it was after three. How had Raju become such a mystery?

She might telephone Arun. But so late at night . . .

At four o'clock Raju was back.

'Where have you been so late? What have you been up to?'

'Mom, I'm tired, let me sleep. Please don't ask any questions.'

*

The flames of the fire are blazing up. They are singing the *mantras* that conclude the sacrificial ritual.

'You didn't go to the office again?'

'I quit my job.'

Guddo was distressed. What was happening to him? Her heart kept pounding.

She had opened Raju's drawer. Bundles of notes . . . where did they all come from? Hundreds, thousands . . . Where did he go with Arun? He's been in jail . . .

Guddo stares into the leaping flames. A strange face, familiar but unfamiliar . . . The face of some defeated superman. Her ears are full of the humming of the flames.

'I have to do something special. Become important. Start my

own company when I have piles of money . . . I'm going to be the president myself.'

'But what's the hurry, Raju? Tell me . . . Such a frantic race! You can get hurt . . . my Raju . . .'

Terrifying flames, a fire engulfing everything. Where has Raju gone astray? Why isn't it clear? That way you'll go crazy . . . stop it, Raju . . .

All the rest of the ingredients for completing the *havan* have been cast into the fire, making the flames crackle still more. Red blue golden flames. Oh Guddo, you thought everybody would be all right, everybody's life would work out right . . . their futures would be bright. Where did it all go? Everything that was tender, fragrant, fresh and pure . . . Radhika's innocent childhood, Raju's brilliant creativity . . . All turned to ashes . . . Who made the ingredients for this *havan*? Had she herself been saved or burned to nothing, like the offerings in the fire?

But the ashes of the sacrificial fire are auspicious, aren't they? Beginnings of new life and new faith . . . the new generations who will spring up here, flourish here, take root in this new earth. Maybe then the demons of loneliness and rootlessness that destroy your identity will finally be turned to ash. Could they really? . . . And these ghosts of selfishness, non-commitment, the frantic materialism . . . could they one day really be turned to ash? . . .

Guddo's eyes are burning from the smoke. Her tears flood over. Those values she has held to with all her faith – has she been able to save them? Will she? And would the desire to save still be there? . . . Is there still any substance left in those values or do they just offer the prop of worn-out rituals? Everything is still burning now, flames and more flames, like the all-engulfing waves of the ocean. Everything burning away . . . Anima, Raju, Tanima, Gita, Radhika . . . and who can say how many others with them.

In the dazzlement of the blaze the ash cannot be seen at all. Sated flames, all golden . . . fragrance . . . smoke . . . black poisonous smoke hovering over more smoke . . . mingling with the flames . . . where is Raju? Guddo suddenly cries out:

'Where are you going, Raju? Stop! Why are you running? . . .'

Glossary

bindi   a cosmetic dot, which may have religious significance or be merely decorative, applied between the eyes

bhajans   popular hymns in Hindi, Braj, etc.

carfare   the money needed for a bus, taxi, etc., especially for travel within a town or city

chaprasi/peon   an errand-boy, messenger, doorman, etc.

charpoy   a cot

chunni   a ceremony in which the bride is given saris, etc.

dharma   the accepted traditional basis (including caste distinctions) for defining a person's religious and social obligations

Divali   the festival of lights, honoring Lakshmi, goddess of beauty and prosperity, and also celebrating Rama's victorious return home

FRCP   Fellow of the Royal College of Physicians

Gayatri   a renowned mantra invoking the sun and recited daily by Hindus

ghi   clarified butter, one of the offerings in the fire sacrifice

gurdvara   a Sikh temple

havan   the ritual fire sacrifice, performed on auspicious occasions and for purification

IAS   Indian Administrative Service, which replaced the Old Indian Civil Service after Independence

jalebi   a sweet made of flour and dal and dipped in syrup

kurta-pajama   long shirt and pants, loose-fitting for men and tight for women

kya?   what?

181

mantra   a religious verse or prayer, often recited as part of a ritual

mehndi   henna, which is applied to the bride's hands and the parting in her hair during the wedding ceremony

paan   betel leaf filled with various spices, chewed as a digestive

pandit   a learned Brahmin, who often officiates as a priest

salwar-qamiz   typical Panjabi women's dress consisting of a long blouse and gathered pants

shagun   an engagement ceremony, preceding the wedding, given by the groom's relatives

Trishanku   a mythical character who was refused entrance into heaven and left suspended between heaven and earth

tulsi   the Indian basil, considered sacred

Vedic mantras   verses from the oldest Sanskrit scriptures

Vedic universities   universities where the Vedas, basic scriptures, are studied